THE LONG ROAD TO LOVING GRAYSON

ALICIA HOPE

ACKNOWLEDGMENTS

This story is written in Australian English.

The situations, organisations and characters in this book are fictional. Any resemblance to an existing or past entity is entirely coincidental.

Lyrics of "Mountain Hideaway" (written and recorded by John Williamson) reproduced with the kind permission of © Emusic Pty Ltd.

DEDICATION

With many thanks to my wonderful husband, Frank, and brilliant sister, Jill. Couldn't have set off on this Long Road without you guys!

ABOUT THE AUTHOR

Once you choose HOPE anything is possible....

Alicia Hope lives on coastal acreage dotted with Australia's famous gum trees and frequented by a delightful variety of birds and animals. Alicia also shares her Queensland home with an author husband, Frank H Jordan, and feathered larrikin, cockatiel Kewbie Kewberton.

Alicia penned *The Long Road to Loving Grayson* after a period of living and working in Cloncurry in remote western Queensland. The idea for the story came to her while out driving – a long road! – one day, and then pestered her until she typed 'The End'.

Writing this novel gave her a chance to re-live the joys of life in outback Queensland, and she hopes readers also enjoy this very Aussie story.

1

Maggie took a sip of her rapidly cooling coffee, grimaced, and sat back to give her latest email one final read-through.

Friday, 7:31:09 AM

From: Maggie.Perkins@MRClonc

To: Regional.Director@MRClonc

Subject: Acting Senior Engineer

Hi Harry, and welcome back from the latest round of meetings in Brisbane. :-)

Grayson Reeves, civil engineer (construction) and our soon-to-be acting senior engineer, emailed yesterday to say he's on his way up from Brisbane. If he has a good run he might call into the office this afternoon.

His relief period officially commences on Monday and I'll greet him on arrival, but I assume you'll want to meet him and discuss the specific tasks he's to concentrate on during his time with us? On that basis I'll arrange a meeting on Monday through Samantha - how's your new PA working out, by the way? I hope you're being nice to her, it's hard finding good people out here you know!

Kind regards,

Maggie

HR Advisor

MR Qld, Cloncurry

=====================

Just another Metro Office engineer coming for a stint of relief work. I wonder what this one'll be like.

Wiping the congealed coffee skin off her lips, she set the cup down on her desk and pushed it well out of the way. Turning back to the computer, she pressed SEND and then submitted a copy of the email to the electronic filing system, her fingers moving over the keyboard and guiding the mouse with practised ease.

She could almost work through the process of appointing relieving staff without thinking. First call for expressions of interest and then assess the EOIs received, submit a recommendation to the relevant supervisor, and finally make an offer to the successful candidate. Or the *only* candidate as was often the case. At least this Grayson character appeared to regard remote service as a chance to see more of the state. Understandable for someone new to the country.

She gave a wry huff. It seemed most staff in Metro or the larger regional offices saw short-term secondment as a penance rather than an opportunity, and were loath to leave the 'safety' of their cushy little cubicles, even temporarily. Then again, who was she to criticise? She'd had her own reservations about moving to the state's remote north west. It had taken weeks of Troy's pleas to make her leave the coast behind, along with all the big city pleasures and conveniences.

Leaning back, she stared thoughtfully at the ceiling. What a surprise it had been to feel an immediate connection with Cloncurry, the little country town that was so far from everywhere else, with its hotter than hot climate and its cordial and colourful characters. At least ... that was what *she'd* experienced on their arrival. Who knows what Troy felt. He never spoke about things like 'feelings'.

Sighing, she called to mind the heartening welcome and *real* friendships she'd found waiting for her here. They'd made the upheaval bearable and even eased the void inside her in a way the lukewarm veneer of city acquaintances never had. And now ... was it even still there, that hollow ache of loss?

She closed her eyes.

Yes, faintly, as though resting between bouts....

When her desk phone jangled she sat forward with a start.

'Cloncurry office, this is Maggie.'

'I've just received an accident report.' The regional director's voice was thick with concern, slicing through the background road noise on his car phone. 'A road train rollover on the Landsborough Highway involving a white dual cab. The caller said the car might've had government plates. Could it be one of our vehicles?'

'Oh no....' She rubbed her forehead. 'We *are* expecting someone, Harry. I just this minute sent you an email about it. Grayson Reeves is travelling up from Brisbane to relieve in the senior engineer's position for six weeks.'

'He's on his way up here now?'

'Left Brisbane yesterday. Where did the accident happen?'

'North of Longreach.'

'How bad?'

'Don't have the details yet. It's only just been reported.'

She frowned. The department was notified of all highway incidents, with rollovers of multi-trailered semis among the most deadly. 'Grayson indicated he'd be taking two days to drive here,' she said slowly, 'so he would've overnighted somewhere along the way.' A thread of tension crept into her voice. 'Half way *would* be around Longreach, or maybe Barcaldine. So I guess it's possible—'

'If he tried to do the fourteen hour journey without a break I'd want to know why,' Harry barked. 'For one thing, he'd be contravening departmental travel policy and fatigue management guidelines.'

'And he's aware of that, Harry. I remind everyone driving long distances of the relevant safety measures, *before* they set off.' She heard a quick exhalation at the other end of the line.

'I know, Maggie, I'm not blaming anyone. I'm just concerned....'

'Understandably, but we could be worrying for nothing.

I'll try to raise Grayson on his mobile but he's likely to be in an area with no reception.'

Harry gave a peeved grunt. 'There are still too many dead spots along the inland highway.'

'So we shouldn't assume the worst if I can't reach him by phone. Once I do get hold of him, I'll let you know straight-away. In the meantime I'm going to think positive. No point worrying 'til we have something to worry about.'

'Yes ... well ... keep me informed.'

After Harry had hung up, Maggie immediately dialled Grayson's mobile number.

'The number you have called is unavailable,' a recorded message said primly. 'The mobile phone is turned off or out of mobile reception range.'

I'll just have to keep trying. Damn the mobile reception out here.

She gave a frustrated sigh.

Think positive, remember?

At a computer ping, she turned back to the screen and opened the incoming email.

Anyone going to the Isa this Saturday?

Her lips tipped upward. There was always someone wanting a lift to Mount Isa on a Saturday, for a spot of shop-ping, socialising, water skiing on Lake Moondara, or just to ease a case of small-town 'cabin fever'. She was rarely able to go on her own, not that she resented the company. Appreciated it, in fact. Troy wasn't big on shopping trips. He also didn't care for the place.

'I don't know why people go to the Isa so often,' he'd muttered in response to her suggestion they take a drive there one Saturday, 'it's ugly. Its most prominent feature is an enormous mine site – makes me feel like I'm at work when I'm there. Nah, I'd rather spend my time here in the Curry.'

Ugly? Maybe ... but without the mine would there even be a town?

Sitting back, she glanced at her wall planner. How long since her last trip to the Isa? Maybe it was time for another one. She smiled, picturing an early morning drive along the Barkly Highway, snaking through rocky terrain where stone formations curved above the earth, their flinty arcs standing out like dinosaurian backbones against the red, gravelly dirt and the brilliant blue of the outback sky.

Her smile faded.

Thinking it might help him enjoy the trip, she had tried sharing her impressions of it with Troy, but her upbeat chatter was met with disinterested grunts or bored silence.

Message received.

The hours passed with no news of Grayson and no reassuring update on the accident. Maggie left messages with the Barcaldine and Winton depots in case Grayson called in there – he sounded the type to want to familiarise himself with the various locations – and tried again and again to raise him on the phone. Her anxiety grew with every unanswered call, and Harry wasn't helping. He kept ringing or dropping into her office to see if she'd heard anything.

In the face of his rising frustration, she thought it prudent to pre-empt what was sure to be his next suggestion. 'I can't bother the police with this, Harry. Grayson's not officially overdue yet.'

'I know,' he replied gruffly, 'and the officers have enough on their plates already, dealing with, and I quote the sergeant in charge, "the distances and other demands of a remote location like this".' He exhaled loudly. 'As if our operations aren't affected by those factors just as much.'

She allowed a silent moment to pass before saying evenly, 'So all we can do is wait for the next update and hope for the best.'

As she watched Harry once more trudge out of her office, Maggie found herself wondering what Grayson would be like. His emails were businesslike though affable, and on the phone his deep voice with its British accent was warm and pleasing to the ear. She pursed her lips. A professional older man perhaps? Or would he surprise her as others had done, by being the complete opposite of what she was expecting?

Probably.

Her lips twitched at the thought of that oh-so-male voice belonging to a scrawny 'Poindexter' type, with squinty eyes behind thickly framed 'Coke-bottle' glasses, pants worn high up under the ribcage, and lily-white lower legs sprouting dark hairs above geeky socks-n-sandals. She gave a shudder and dismissed the cringe-worthy image.

It doesn't matter what he looks like as long as he arrives

safely and can do the job.

With a decisive nod, she turned her attention to the paperwork on her desk.

Right, back to it....

A few hours later, the receptionist poked her head around the door to Maggie's office. 'There's a big guy in reception asking for you, Mags. It's that new relief engineer.'

Grayson!

She jumped to her feet. 'Oh, thank goodness! Could you make sure Harry knows he's arrived safely please?'

'I'll go and tell Samantha.' The receptionist hurried away, calling for someone to mind the front desk for a few minutes.

Realising Grayson would find it strange if she raced out to meet him gushing a welcome, Maggie took a moment to tuck a stray wisp of hair behind an ear, smooth her crisp white blouse, and straighten her tailored trousers.

We might be 'out bush', she told herself for the umpteenth time, but there's no need to look like a 'bushy'.

Reaching down to grasp her computer mouse, she closed the complicated workforce planning spreadsheet she'd been staring at in the hope a solution might jump out at her. It hadn't, at least not yet. She shook her head. It was always stressful trying to balance managers' requests for additional staff with budgeted workforce allocations, especially when some managers didn't understand – or chose to ignore – the restrictions placed on Public Service appointments.

I'll get back to that later. A fresh eye might help me see

something I've missed.

Striding out of her office, she rounded the corner to reception and stopped in her tracks. The man standing patiently waiting on the other side of the counter was certainly no Poindexter. Tall and well built, he looked to be in his early thirties, not much older than Maggie herself.

Why did I expect an older man? The deepness of his voice maybe....

The young woman manning reception glanced at her and announced in a loud whisper, 'Says his name's Grey something or other.'

Maggie saw the shadow of a grin cross his face and sighed inwardly.

Honestly, some of the trainees we get out here....

Throwing him an apologetic glance, she leaned down to say quietly to the stand-in, 'It's Grayson, Leticia, and good receptionists develop tools to get visitors' names right so they can be announced properly.'

The young woman looked sheepish and flashed the visitor a rueful glance.

Straightening, Maggie turned to him with a bright smile and found him gazing intently at her.

'Maggie?'

There it is, that deep voice....

Skirting the counter, she strode up to him, hand extended. 'Yes, Grayson, nice to meet you.' She couldn't help adding in a gush, 'I'm *so* pleased to see you.' When this earned her an amused frown, she cleared her throat. 'Pleased you made it safely.'

As she spoke her hand was grasped in a firm, warm grip with – thankfully – no hint of finger crush, and his grey-flecked hazel eyes gazed at her with friendly interest. The shape of the dark brows above them made his wide face appear serious, even a little stern.

And then he smiled.

Charisma, how nice! Makes a change from the charm-challenged engineering types we normally get. And a real handshake too, not one of those horrid 'boneless fish' versions.

Tick and tick.

Noticing the unspoken question in his eyes, she said hastily, 'We were worried you might've been involved in a highway accident north of Longreach. I tried and tried to get you on your mobile—'

'An accident?' There was that frown again. 'I didn't see one. Must've happened after I passed through there.'

'The report said one of the vehicles might've been a Government car, so you can imagine our concern.'

'Oh, right. The fleet vehicle I drove up doesn't have a mobile phone recharger, and wouldn't you know it, my battery went flat half way.' He threw her a rueful grin. 'I'm sorry to have caused unnecessary worry.'

'No probs, what's important is that you're here, safe and sound.' Maggie beamed up at him. 'And you've chosen a good day to arrive. It's pay week Friday, so we'll all be heading to the Stubby Hut after work.'

'I think you mentioned that. Run by your social club, isn't it?'

She nodded.

'Why is it called a hut?'

'After the soils laboratory was relocated from what they'd affectionately, or not-so-affectionately,' and she gave an amused huff, 'christened "the hut", it was allocated to the club for use as a base. The committee did a great job with the renovations, transforming the worn-out ex-lab into a quirky nightspot. Now it's open to members and friends every second Friday. The club serves cut-price drinks and barbeque meals, and organises pool and darts comps, car rallies, that sort of thing. They're also in charge of our end of year functions.'

'That's grand. I'm glad I got here on the right day, I could use a cold lager after the long trip. Can hardly speak over all the dust in my throat.' As he spoke his lips tilted in a wide grin. He had even, white teeth and a strong mouth that smiled easily.

Maggie returned the smile.

We might've scored a good one here.

Behind the desk Leticia sat idly watching the pair, noting that Maggie, of above average height herself, had to look up at Grayson. As she ran her eyes over him, Leticia tapped her chin with a finger.

He was a big dude alright. Looked to be in this thirties, *way* too old to interest her. Anyway she had a boyfriend, and compared to Grayson he was....

More like a weasel than a warrior?

Her brow creased and she hastily dropped her gaze.

2

___

'So, Grayson, it looked like you enjoyed yourself on Friday night.'

'I did. Everyone was right friendly.'

At his sheepish glance Maggie grinned. 'Yeah ... new starters tend to cause something of a stir.'

Especially someone like Grayson who, at six foot four, stood out among the Stubby Hut crowd.

Finance officer Peta had noticed him as soon as he appeared.

Intent on making the most of her temporary freedom from husband and kids, she had arrived early. Dancing up to the bar singing, 'Let's get this party started,' she downed her first drink after raising it in a quick toast to Friday nights. Slamming the empty shot glass onto the bar with a satisfied, 'Ahh,' she immediately ordered another two, and two more after that.

The sweetened alcohol hit her empty stomach with a gratifying fizz, before boogying along her veins to reach her head, fingers, and toes.

By the time Grayson turned up Peta was on her fifth drink, and buzzing. She spied him making his way to the bar and froze with her glass mid-way to her open mouth. A blurry instant later, having dropped the half-empty glass on the bar and spilling its contents, to the barman's annoyance, she slipped down from her barstool.

After taking a moment to steady herself, she pushed off the bar to shoulder through the crowd with the focused determination of an attacking great white shark.

Positioning herself well within Grayson's comfort zone she gazed tipsily up at him. "N you are...?' Without giving him time to answer she launched into a slurred account of her own vital statistics, clumsily avoiding any mention of marital status.

Maggie watched the scene unfold from where she stood talking to Harry and his wife, and when Peta swayed even closer to put a hand on Grayson's arm, Maggie wondered how he'd react.

Would he be a gentleman about the booze-fuelled advances or an insensitive cad?

The former, she decided, judging by Peta's longing rather than resentful expression when he manoeuvred his way out of 'danger'.

Eagle-eyed Tom Gilmore had helped on that score, by waving a pool cue in the air and calling, 'Hey, tall dude. C'mon, it's your shot.'

Tom to the rescue, once again.

And now it was Monday morning, Grayson's first day on the job. He sat at ease in Maggie's visitor's chair, long legs stretched in front of him and the ankles of his work-booted feet crossed.

'So, apart from giving us all a scare,' she said with a wry smile, 'did you enjoy the trip up from Brisbane?'

He nodded. 'Although it was awfully long, as you warned it would be. Guess I'll get used to Australia's distances. Was great seeing the country's heart instead of hugging the coast, which is pretty much what I've been doing since I arrived.'

'How long have you been in Australia?'

'About ten months now.'

'You're on a Four Five Seven visa?' Even in casual conversation Maggie couldn't help slipping into business mode. It was where she felt safest.

'That's right. I've just started my three-year stint and can't believe how quickly the time is going.'

'You must be enjoying it here, then.'

'How right you are.' He smiled. 'This is a great place. Not that the "old country" wasn't, but there's a freshness about Australia you don't get anywhere else. Must be all the blue sky and sunshine. And no long, dreary winters to endure.'

'Yes, well, out here it's about as fresh – if you can call it that – as it gets, and more blue sky and sunshine than you could ever want.' They shared a grin and she handed him a booklet. 'Now I guess we'd better get going on your induction. Don't feel singled out, every new arrival has to put up with this.'

'I'm sure I'll survive.'

Did she imagine it, or was there a warm chocolate coating on those words and a twinkle in the eyes smiling into hers? With an inward frown at herself, she launched into the all-too-familiar induction spiel. When she saw Grayson sit forward in his chair to rest his arms on his bent knees and gaze levelly at her, she felt a rush of gratitude. He was actually listening!

She sensed he was still paying attention when a short while later he ran a large hand through his close-cropped sandy hair and lowered his gaze. She took the opportunity to look him over.

Tall, well built, and with an outdoorsy tan – his skin no doubt transformed from British lily-white by the Queensland sun – he had what her best friend Evie would describe as a real man's figure. His dark polo shirt clung a little to a well-rounded chest and muscular arms, and skimmed over a flat stomach. He wore his blue jeans low – but not too low – on a set of lean hips.

She gave an mental nod of satisfaction.

No 'undies-out-the-top' for this bloke.

It was easy to imagine what Evie would say about him.

'Wooh ... he's got the classic V shape, Mags! And doesn't look like one of those maybe-I'm-a-man-and-maybe-I'm-not metrosexual types, nah-ah. *This* is a man who could hold even a strong girl close and make her feel safe.'

When he raised his head to once more meet her eyes, Maggie revised her first impression of him. Grayson didn't have a stern disposition, just a focused, resolute nature. One highly suited to an engineer.

She smiled. 'Right, that's it. Boring diatribe over. You're a good listener, Grayson, makes a nice change from most newbies who can't wait to get away from me – until there's a problem with their pay that is.'

He gave a slow smile. 'I didn't find it boring by any means.'

Marvelling again at how the smile transformed his face, she was also disquieted by her response to it.

The warm, delicious sensation that was somehow also ... dangerous.

She pushed those thoughts aside and rose to her feet. 'Right, I'll introduce you to the other staff.'

As they made their way through the office, Maggie noticed the young – and some not so young – women fussing over their hair and clothes. Easy-on-the-eye and young-enough-to-be-interesting men like Grayson rarely graced the office corridors, so when one came along, especially one with a deliciously Colin Firth-like voice, some preening was to be expected.

Maggie's lips twitched and she flicked him a glance from under her lashes. While not classically handsome, Grayson radiated masculinity and strength of character, and had an air of intelligence about him.

It's early days, she reminded herself. Who knows what he's like when not on his best behaviour.

She hastily focused her gaze forward when he turned to her and asked, 'Engineering next?'

'If you like.'

'I'm keen to meet my work team.'

'Good for you. We'll go straight there.'

Everyone in the Engineering section quickly gathered on their arrival, eager to eyeball the 'new boy' who was to be their relieving senior.

'I'll leave you with this lot, Grayson.' Turning to the group, Maggie admonished with mock severity, 'Look after him, you blokes, so he might consider coming to work with us again.' She glanced back at Grayson. 'You know where my office is. My door's always open if you need anything.'

'Thanks, Maggie. Good to know I can call on you while I'm finding my way around.' This earned Grayson some barely-disguised smirks.

She ignored them. 'Glad to help any way I can. We want you to enjoy your time with us. We're always looking for good engineers up here.' After flashing him a winning smile she turned on her heel to leave, only to stop and slap a palm to her forehead. Whirling around, she thrust out a hand to gain Grayson's attention. When it came into contact with his shirtfront instead of his arm she hastily jerked her hand back, but not before registering the solid beat of his heart and the firm, warm strength of his chest beneath her fingers.

'Oh! I....' She struggled to keep her voice steady. It didn't help that he was gazing at her with a hint of amused sympathy in his eyes. 'I ... nearly forgot.' She swallowed. 'I'm planning a trip to the gulf to visit one of our crews and Harry suggested you might like to come along.' Her cheeks burned at the breathiness in her voice. She cleared her throat. 'He believes having engineers visit remote sites is good for staff morale, and it would give you a chance to see "coal-face" operations up there.'

'Right you are. Just let me know when.'

With a breezy, 'Great. It'll probably be some time in the next few weeks,' she dipped her head at him before turning to stride back toward her office.

Grayson watched her go. She had a graceful long-legged gait and held her head high as she walked, the mane of dark hair hanging down her back neatly pinned in a silver clasp. Her corporate-wear white blouse and navy trousers sat easily on a set of square shoulders, straight back, narrow hips and firm derriere.

When she stopped a short way along the corridor for a quick word with a colleague, he studied her profile. Her finely drawn face was well-proportioned and feminine, with high cheek bones, a long, straight nose, full lips, and a precise jaw line. The pretty blush that had infused her cheeks a few moments ago lingered as a rose-pink tint under her clear skin.

A voice from behind snapped him out of his pleasant scrutiny. 'So, Grayson, if you can take your eyes off Maggie's arse for a minute, what's your story? Not that we blame you for checking her out, of course. We've all done it.'

Turning, he gazed into the curious faces of the engineers who would be his work team for the next six weeks. They stared back at him, some smirking roguishly. He raised a nonchalant eyebrow. 'My story? Well chaps, I've been with the department for about ten months now, in Metro office in Brisbane. Before that I was living in the UK where I worked as a senior engineer in civil construction. So I have a lot of engineering experience but am still getting to know the Australian environment.'

'Yeah, well you'll get more "environment" out this way then you could ever want, mate!' The speaker's exaggerated Australian drawl was greeted by a group chuckle as he went on. 'And I see you're gettin' to know the Aussie sheilas while you're at it. Fancy havin' the prospect of a road trip with our lovely Maggie, and after only being here for five minutes. How lucky can one bloke be?'

Triumph crinkled the corners of Grayson's eyes but his expression stiffened when the speaker added, 'Shame she's married, mate.'

He hadn't thought to check her ring finger.

Hang on ... why was he even thinking this?

He swallowed a scowl.

'So you're an "intoh" then?' another in the group piped up. At Grayson's uncertain expression, he explained, 'That's what we call international recruits, like our mate Chandra here,' and he indicated a slightly built man at the back of the group. 'He arrived this year from Nepal with his new – and I mean, all of five minutes married – bride.'

Grayson nodded a greeting at the shyly grinning Chandra as someone else asked, 'So are you just doing your three years, or are you planning to stay in Australia?'

He took a moment to answer. 'That was the plan, to emigrate to Australia and start a new life here.'

'On your own?'

This met with a quick frown. 'It turned out that way.'

'Oh yeah?'

'Yeah.' Taking a breath, Grayson said with a lopsided grin, 'Anyway chaps, how about *I* ask the questions now?'

3

As she strode along the empty main street, Maggie glanced at the digital clock mounted high on the pale brick façade of the historic town hall. The 07:05 time display clicked over to show the current temperature, a pleasant twenty-nine degrees Celsius. She smiled, grateful for autumn's respite from summer's high forties to low fifties temperatures, which would return all too soon.

Approaching the office building, she was surprised to see a light glowing from a window in the engineering section. After letting herself inside she dumped her bag in her office, collected her coffee cup, and went down the corridor to poke her head around the door to the senior's office.

When he caught sight of her Grayson put down the schematic he'd been studying and leaned back in his chair, smiling a greeting.

'What do we have here?' She grinned and stepped into

the room. 'Another early starter? I'm used to having the whole building – actually, the whole town pretty much! – to myself first thing in the mornings.'

'Oh? Have I broken some unwritten rule?' His eyes danced at her. They looked a smoky grey colour in the morning light.

'Not at all. It's great to see you so keen to get started. And speaking of getting started, I'm heading for the staff room to make myself a 'heart-starter' coffee. Would you like one?'

'Sure, I'll have another cup. Usually it's tea.' At her raised eyebrows he gave a chuckle. 'I'm British, remember? To us tannin is the sixth food group. I'm not properly awake until I've had my first ...,' and he accentuated his British accent, '... cup-a-char.' Rising to his feet, he collected a large black mug bearing the inscription *I'm here and I'm awake ... what more do you want?* from off the desk. 'I'll come and make it myself.'

Seeing her amused glance at the mug he gave a sheepish half-smile. 'I take this old thing wherever I go, out of habit. It was a gift from my wife ... er ... ex-wife. That was before—' His eyes stopped dancing and his expression tightened. When Maggie looked at him curiously, the words tumbled from his mouth. 'We were all set to emigrate together, only she had second thoughts. Left me at Heathrow Airport as we were about to board the plane to Sydney.'

Maggie saw a ripple of bitterness cross his face and resisted the impulse to touch a comforting hand to his arm. Had he been a woman, or an older man perhaps ... or if the idea of touching him didn't feel ... precarious ... somehow....

She shoved that thought aside. 'I'm so sorry, Grayson. How long had you been married?'

'A bit over two years, and together for a few before that.' Taking a breath, he added in a firm, let's-move-on tone, 'Such is life, as that famous Aussie once said. The move to Australia didn't give me time to mope and it offered us both a fresh start. So I guess it wasn't all bad.'

Brave words, but when he looked at her Maggie saw pain lingering deep in his eyes, along with something akin to anger. At himself perhaps, for mentioning a painful subject?

'Well, if it's any consolation, we're glad that you – and your cup – still came.' She gave an encouraging smile and was pleased to see his expression lift. As they made their way into the staff kitchen she said briskly, 'Now, I won't promise the tea bags or instant coffee here are the best but they're all we've got. At least the water's hot.'

He nodded, helped himself to a tea bag from the jar on the counter, and then lined up beside Maggie to wait his turn for the hot water. He gazed down at her bent head and caught the scent of her perfume. It was fresh, unobtrusive, with a soft strength of character.

Like her.

Beside him, Maggie spooned dark coffee grains into her mug, covered them with a generous splash of cold milk, and then topped the blend with boiling water from a tap in the sink marked VERY HOT in red letters. After a vigorous stir which left a creamy swirl of froth on top, she took a sip to check for taste, leaving a tiny white moustache clinging to her full top lip. When she deftly erased the froth with a flick of her tongue, Grayson hastily turned away.

As the harsh midday sun glinted off a passing car's windscreen, Grayson turned to eye the man in the driver's seat beside him, fellow engineer and 'quasi-local' Tom Gilmore. Tom enjoyed a chat at the best of times, and wasn't about to let slip the opportunity to 'grill' his acting senior while on a familiarisation drive around the region.

'So, mate, you got any rellies here in Oz?'

'No, my parents and brother are all in the UK.'

'How do you stay in touch with them?'

'Phone and online.'

'What'd we do before the internet, hey?'

Grayson nodded.

'So, what does your brother do? Is he an engineer too?'

Grayson paused before answering. 'The plan was for Mark to follow me into the field ... well, Dad's plan anyway. He's always had high expectations of us. Considers career success the defining mark of a man.'

'I see.' Tom picked up the acrimonious note in Grayson's voice. 'How far off is Mark from graduating?'

'A long way off, as it happens.' Grayson turned to once more gaze out the window. 'He dropped out of university part-way through his undergraduate engineering degree ... to pursue a career in horticulture.'

'Horticulture? That's a big shift in professions. How did your father take the news?'

Grayson gave a derisive snort. 'Not well. Abandoning a promising career to be what he calls a "low down, grubby gardener" makes Mark a loser, according to dear old Dad.'

'That's a bit harsh.'

'Yes, well ... when he's not happy, our father makes sure everyone knows it.' Grayson sighed. 'And I have to accept part of the blame for his ill temper.'

'How's that?'

'My marriage broke down around the time Mark dropped out, and I think Dad felt like both his sons were failures. He was most disappointed with Mark but was also royally upset about me and Tina, which is ironic when I think about it.' Grayson flicked Tom a glance. 'He'd started calling her "Little Miss Hoity-Toity", and warned me her expensive tastes would break me if I didn't take them in hand. It's a wonder he didn't revel in the old "I told you so" when things went sour.'

He gave a grim smile and rubbed a large hand over his chin. 'I'm more fortunate than Mark, though. I have distance on my side, and a successful career Dad respects. I'm afraid Mark gets to bear the brunt of Dad's displeasure at *both* our "failures". It's a real shame 'cos my little brother's always had a green thumb, and I reckon he has the nous to succeed in horticulture.' Grayson turned away again. 'I've tried telling Dad that but the stubborn old coot refuses to listen, so my only other option for helping Mark from way over here was to provide some financial backing for his nursery venture.

Left me a bit short, especially after the divorce settlement, but this is my brother I'm talking about.'

Grayson blinked and swallowed, and Tom noticed him stiffen, as though self-conscious at having revealed so much to a virtual stranger. With his gaze on the road ahead, Tom asked, 'So is your marriage kaput or will we have the pleasure of meeting the hoity-toity Tina some time?'

'Kaput,' Grayson said flatly, '*absolutely* kaput.' He paused before going on. 'Anyhow that's my story, and probably more than you wanted to know. So what about you? Got family here?'

'Yep, you're lookin' at one lucky bloke. I was smart enough to slap a ring on Lisa's finger soon after meetin' her.' He threw Grayson a wink. 'I've been glad of that ever since. And now we have two beaut kids.' His grin broadened. 'Gotta pinch myself sometimes.'

'Good for you, cobber.'

The men shared an indulgent moment and then Tom said, 'I'll tell you who else is a lucky bloke, only Troy Kerr doesn't realise it.' He squinted at Grayson. 'That's Maggie's husband.'

'Oh, right.' Grayson sat straighter in his seat. 'So what's the story there?'

'Well, Maggie's what you Poms might call a "right cracker". Clever, capable, and easy on the eye ... as I think you've already noticed?' When Grayson shifted uneasily in his seat Tom raised an amused eyebrow. 'Lisa and I have known her for quite a while now. She's a good friend and a lovely person, but we find it hard – *real* hard – to like her hubby.

Look, why don't I just come out and say it. Troy Kerr is a pratt. Dull as dog poo and dumb enough to take a good sort like Maggie for granted.' Shaking his head, he growled, 'The fool doesn't deserve her.'

'Hang on ... did you say Kerr? Isn't Maggie's surname Perkins?'

'She kept her maiden name when they married. Hey, speaking of names, I hope you won't mind if the blokes don't call you "Grayson". Knowing them, it'll be Reevers, or Gray, or something like that. They don't mean any disrespect, it's just the Aussie way.'

'No bother.' Grayson shrugged a broad shoulder. 'I've been called worse.'

'I bet you have.' Tom chuckled and then grew serious as he pointed through the windscreen. 'See up ahead? That's the road re-seal I was telling you about....'

After taking Grayson past two more job sites, he turned the car around. 'That's about all I can show you for now. The other projects are a day's drive or further away.'

'Thanks Tom.'

'Anytime.'

They travelled in companionable silence for a while and then Grayson looked across at him. 'I'm curious. Why did you say Maggie's husband doesn't deserve her?'

Tom accelerated to overtake a loaded cattle truck before answering. 'I guess each to his own and all that, and no one can blame a young bloke for wantin' to get ahead financially, but Kerr works every double shift he can and then spends most of his down-time out pig-hunting or at the pub.' He gave a disapproving shake of his head. 'Leaving a hotty like Maggie on her own so much, especially in a small community with a large proportion of single men, is *not* the move of a smart man.'

'No.' Grayson stared moodily out the window.

'Don't get me wrong, I don't think Kerr's a *bad* person, he's just thoughtless, "insensitive" as my Lisa would say, and short a few roos in the top paddock. That means dumb,' and Tom tapped his temple with a finger. 'I overheard him at a work function once, tellin' the regional director everything he was doin' wrong in managing the region's roads – can you believe it? I was so embarrassed for Maggie. It's no wonder she goes to most functions on her own now.'

He squinted at Grayson. 'If you're wondering how someone like her could've hooked up with a loser like him in the first place you wouldn't be alone. Lisa reckons it was a misplaced sense of obligation on Maggie's part. See her parents died in a car accident, and after that she got sort of obsessed with making their every wish come true. Apparently at one stage they'd hoped she and Troy might get together, for some reason I can't fathom.' Tom accelerated again, this time to overtake a motorhome spewing smoke from its exhaust. He eyed it as they passed, muttering, 'That poor rig's seen better days.'

Grayson gave a distracted grunt.

'Anyhow, if you ask me, Kerr took advantage of her at a

vulnerable time, which I guess is the main reason I can't like or respect the bloke.'

The crease deepened in Grayson's brow. 'Married life can be pretty wretched if shared with the wrong person. Better to be alone than a miserable half of a miserable whole.'

Even if freedom came at a hefty price, as it had for him.

Recalling the moment his life and vision of the future shattered in Heathrow's departure lounge, he sighed.

If only he'd known what was going on behind his back he would've dealt with it, maybe even nipped it in the bud. But would the end result have been the same, regardless? Probably. Where there's smoke....

So while he may not have ended up in Australia, in all likelihood he would still have ended up alone.

Hang on ... something was different.

He frowned.

Where was the sting that usually accompanied thoughts on that subject?

Searching inside himself, he discovered a new sense of detachment. Was he finally managing to put the gut-wrenching episode behind him, to collect the shards of his life and glue them back in place? Had time stepped up to its role of world's best healer?

Or do some wounds go too deep to ever fully heal?

4

Maggie had the receiver wedged between a smooth cheek and shoulder when Grayson appeared in her doorway. She raised a beckoning hand and he dipped his head in thanks as he stepped inside. Taking a seat he leaned forward, resting his elbows on his knees and clasping his hands together between them. While Maggie continued speaking into the phone, he watched her capable fingers race over the keyboard and columns of figures scroll in a blur across the computer screen.

'You're welcome. Let me know how you get on.' After hanging up, she turned and caught a look of open admiration in her visitor's gaze. 'Hello, Grayson. How was your first week?'

'Good.' His mouth split into a wide smile. 'It's a great team you have up here, all right friendly and helpful.'

'Glad to hear it. Positive feedback can be hard to get. We

often only hear about problems – you know, the old "no news is good news".'

'Ah yes, that old chestnut.'

They grinned together.

'So what can I do for you this morning?'

'Just wanted to drop by and check I'm meeting expectations.'

'Conscientious of you.' She gave an approving nod. 'Well, I can tell you that Harry's pleased with how you've settled in, and the progress on projects you've made in a short time. And from all accounts you've also won the respect of the other engineers.'

'Good to know. Harry's easy to get along with as far as bosses go, and the engineers are a fine bunch.'

Maggie smiled. 'And what about Cloncurry? How are you finding the place?'

'It's not a bad little village.'

Her grin widened.

'And I'm getting used to the heat and dust.'

'Ah yes, two things I won't be sorry to leave behind when we eventually return to "civilisation". Though I can't complain, we have it pretty good, really.' She sat back in her chair. 'I miss having a garden, though.'

'You can't have one here?'

'Plants have to be tough to survive these conditions. All the care in the world couldn't save the ones I brought from the coast, the scorching sun and unrelenting heat was too much for them.' Her face fell. 'I knew it was a gamble bringing Mum's potted rose, but I just couldn't bear to part with it.' There was a quiver in her voice. 'Of course later I wished I *had* left it behind when it bloomed one final, desperate time, before withering in front of my eyes....'

She swallowed, blinked, and forced a smile. 'It took me a while to realise that there *is* life and beauty out here, merely hidden beneath the dust. It happened when I saw the brittle skeleton of a what I thought was a long dead bougainvillea burst into glossy green leaves and bright puce blossoms after a shower of rain. It was a simply breathtaking display. So, while there are hardships to living out here, there are also surprising wonders if you take the time to look.'

Grayson eyed her for a long moment before speaking. 'What about your husband? Does he feel the same way about being here?'

'Not quite.' She gave a wry huff. 'It's ironic really. Troy instigated the move but took longer to adapt to our new life-style. Oh sure, he enjoys the additional "rural and remote" benefits attached to my public service position and his week-on, week-off job with Red Rock Mine, but grizzles like crazy when the temperature goes over forty degrees Celsius. And with Cloncurry claiming Australia's highest ever recorded temperature, that happens a lot.'

She didn't add the other irony, that the extreme tempera-tures he claimed to hate didn't stop Troy from going on regular hunting trips, where he and his mates had to rough-it in the bush for days on end.

Grayson nodded his understanding. 'Can I ask something else not work-related?'

'Of course.'

'I've noticed a strange smell coming into my motel unit at night, one I can't quite place.'

Maggie's eyes held a flicker of amusement. 'Is it an unpleasant, sort of chemical smell? Similar to bottled gas?'

He nodded.

'Then that'll be gidgee weed, which I think is coming into season about now.'

'Gidgee weed?'

'A plant peculiar to this area, or so I believe. The plants flower after rain and release their "perfume", typically during the night. I didn't know what to make of the cloying stench either at first, and even after someone enlightened me, I couldn't believe such an unnatural smell could originate from the flowers of an otherwise innocuous plant.'

He pulled a face. 'It's certainly in a class all its own.' He paused while they shared another grin and then said, 'Say, the chaps ... er ... blokes told me there's some kind of big event happening here this weekend. "Shindig" I think they called it.'

'I see you're being coached in Aussie-isms.'

'Too right.' His grey eyes crinkled at the corners.

His attempt at an Aussie accent made her smile. 'Good for you. And yes, the annual Cloncurry rodeo's on this weekend. It's a big deal for the region. Like the racing carnival and district show, the rodeo's held in the cooler months as people venture out of air-conditioned hibernation. So, I hope you brought along some riding boots and an Akubra hat?'

'I did bring a hat but I don't own a pair of riding boots. I hope these will suffice.' He stretched out a long, blue-jeaned leg to reveal a leather work boot.

She gave it a quick scan. Its scuffed ruggedness suited his manly persona rather well. 'They'll be fine.' Her eyebrows twitched. 'And the steel caps will protect your toes from any dance-related injuries.'

'Dancing?'

'You bet! People out here like to squeeze the fun-juice out of every event, so there's a "knees-up" in the hall on Saturday night.'

He gave an amused grunt.

'The fun kicks off this afternoon with a street parade,' she went on, 'and then people tend to gravitate to one of the pubs for dinner. The rodeo is on all weekend, followed next Saturday by the first race meeting of the season. You'll see all the moths and glad rags come out of the wardrobes for that one.' She liked the way his eyes tilted upward at the corners when he was amused.

'Will you be going to all the events?'

'I expect so.'

Socialising with newbies after hours was an important part of her job. It helped them settle in, especially the more introverted ones. Although Grayson didn't strike her as the needy type....

'Well then, I'll probably see you at this afternoon's parade.' He rose and smiled down at her.

'You probably will.' As she returned the smile their eyes made a firm connection, and she felt something flow between them, a sensation she couldn't classify. And then her phone shrilled again, breaking the moment.

Grayson gave her a parting wave as he strode out.

Standing in the shade of a gritty street tree that afternoon, Maggie waved away the odd fly as she watched the gaudy floats begin their slow, noisy procession around the town's main streets. Troy had opted not to join her, saying it was still too hot to venture out of the air conditioning, for which she'd been secretly pleased.

More often than not he managed to spoil things, and not only for her.

The disloyalty of that thought jabbed her and she winced. Bending her head, she watched an ant scurrying about in what seemed like a pointless fashion around the tree's base. What was it doing? Trying to build a nest? If so, it wasn't getting far.

Her lips tightened.

Futile endeavours ... I know how they feel, little ant.

She recalled staring down at her engagement ring, face aglow, shortly after Troy slipped it on her finger, and felt her insides clench. At the time she'd pictured her future like a well-tended garden bed ready to spring into life and blossom, only to see her incompatibility with her husband drain the life from those early shoots like the hot north-western sun on tender seedlings, leaving the garden empty and barren.

She scowled and scuffed the toe of a boot over the dusty pavement.

Evie had been right.

In typical style she hadn't bothered to hide her dismay at her friend's choice of life partner, leaving Maggie wordlessly gaping at her impassioned outburst. But then Evie was a McGuire, and like the rest of her quirky family, famous for her robust personality and gauche call-it-like-it-is approach to life. Unlike most people, Maggie found her refreshing and stimulating company. That day, however, after Evie gasped at the glint of diamonds on Maggie's ring finger, she had felt the full force of her friend's indelicate tongue.

'Oh Mags, *no.*' Evie had stared at her with wide, appalled eyes. 'Tell me you haven't done something stupid.' At Maggie's guilty silence, she groaned. 'No, no, *no.* It was never meant to come to *this.* He was just a date night, a fling to cheer you up, or did you forget that?' She threw her hands in the air. 'You're *completely* wrong for each other. Just 'cos your families were friends, that's not enough reason to *marry* the guy! You've said yourself the two of you didn't have much to do with each other over the years. And no wonder, you have *nothing* in common!'

Reaching out to grasp Maggie's arms, Evie had glared into her eyes and said slowly, as though to drive the message home, 'We're talking *marriage* here, *forever* stuff.' She frowned. 'Well ... maybe not forever for everyone, but it *would* be for you, knowing your over-active do-the-right-thing gene.' Pausing, she gave Maggie a shake. 'Troy's a nega-tive, mind-numbing, intellectual vacuum. He's not bad looking, I'll give you that, but let's face it, Mags, his bad qualities outweigh the few good ones he has. Surely you can see that?'

She released her grip and let her hands fall. 'You're a gorgeous, well-liked, smart career woman, and there's a wonderful Mr Right for you out there. Don't cut him out of the picture by chaining yourself to Mr Wrong! And if ever there was a Mr Wrong for you, it's Troy Kerr.' When Maggie made as if to protest Evie went on stoutly, 'I could never forgive myself if I didn't try to talk my BFF out of doing something she'd regret for the rest of her life.'

Thrusting both hands on her hips, she frowned into Maggie's face. 'Are you sure you're not grasping at happiness because you're in a vulnerable place right now? It's not long since you lost your parents, and I know how much they meant to you. That emotional toll can affect decision-making, and for quite a while too.'

Evie's advice was well-intentioned but it had re-kindled the old pain. The sudden loss of her parents, the only people with whom she could drop the professional veneer and be her real self, had left Maggie rocked by shock and grief. Their loss had torn a gaping hole in her life, a wretched inner chasm that time could only ever cover, never fully heal.

Their loving influence had injected sanity back into her sometimes intense life, so with them gone, she had to seek that calming influence elsewhere. It had seemed fortuitous that when her parents' friends, the Kerrs, called to pay their respects, they brought their son with them.

Troy.

His attentiveness and steadying – Evie would say

'tedious' – influence while Maggie handled the funeral and other heartrending arrangements had been a balm to her frayed emotions. It brought to mind the hints her parents had dropped about him in the early days. And so his proposal, mere weeks after the funeral, had felt like a yellow brick road out of Grief Central.

And then came their wedding day, what she now thought of as the precursor to disaster.

Maggie squeezed her eyes shut but the memory continued playing.

First, pouring rain had forced the wedding party to splash through puddles as they charged, dripping, into the church. And then her eyes had alighted on the empty spaces in the church's front pew normally assigned to the proud parents of the bride – spaces she had specifically requested *not* be set aside – and tears had mixed with the raindrops on her face.

Later, at the wedding breakfast, some clumsy oaf – one of Troy's mates – bumped the wedding cake table and the porcelain bride and groom decoration on top of the cake crashed to the floor, smashing into pieces before everyone's horrified eyes. And when Maggie, by now going through the motions with gritted teeth, obeyed tradition and threw her bouquet of white roses into the air, they slipped through all the outstretched fingers to fall to the scuffed dance floor, where they became a pathetic little pile of trampled leaves, damp blooms and crumpled satin ribbon.

That was the last straw for bridesmaid Evie. Choking back a sob, she had bundled up the filmy layered skirt of her gown and rushed to the ladies, hot tears of sympathy for her friend coursing down her cheeks. Witnessing Evie's tearful exit, Maggie had to swallow her own tears and plaster a smile on her face, knowing it was too late to change her mind, and determined that nothing would stop her granting her parents' wish.

It didn't take long for her to realise what a big mistake she'd made, rushing into marriage with a man she barely knew. Troy's emotional and intellectual contributions to their relationship – not huge in the first place – pretty much dried up as soon as they left the wedding reception, and when a while later she cautiously suggested they work on getting to know each other better, he'd been affronted.

'We've known each other for years and now we're *married*, yet you're saying we're still *strangers*? Well that's just great. I do you a good turn and this is how you thank me. Talk about ungrateful.' He raised a hand when she made to speak and barked, 'Discussion over,' before stalking off.

And now she was two years into a marriage that felt more and more like a miserable life sentence. While acknowledging that brought on the usual pinch of guilt, there was no denying the fact she didn't love or respect her husband, not in the way she'd envisaged cherishing the man in her life. But she had taken Troy for better or worse, and her pride, sense of duty, and an obligation born of love for her parents, would see her honour that commitment.

Maggie sighed. At least he wasn't interested in having children ... yet ... and her job brought a measure of satisfaction and fulfilment to her life, along with as much social interaction with her workmates and their partners as she could ever want. And Troy was away a lot, allowing her to be herself, or someone like herself, most of the time....

A sudden shout close-by startled her. On a passing float, the school principal was calling out her name and holding up sweets to throw her way. She was laughing, waving and dodging flying lollies when Grayson walked up to stand beside her.

She grinned a welcome at him and chuckled, 'I'm being showered in sweet booty!'

'Well, we mustn't let it go to waste. Or should that be w-a-i-s-t?' His laugh, like his voice, was deep and warm, and made feather-like tingles run up and down her spine.

When he bent to help her collect the sweets scattered on the ground, she took in his slim-fitting cream moleskin pants, tan leather belt, chambray shirt, and classic, under-stated brown Akubra hat. The brim was tilted over his eyes, slate-grey eyes regarding her with an amused gleam in their depths.

'So, do I pass?'

'Oh yes.' She hadn't meant the words to sound so breathy. Clearing her throat, she straightened and said crisply, 'You definitely look the part.'

He also smelled good, fresh and woodsy, but she kept that to herself.

'Why thank you, ma'am.' He was openly grinning at her now, and she couldn't resist a snicker at his bad Texan accent tinged with an unavoidable Britishness.

For his part, he had taken her in from across the road –

no hat, well cut Western-style blue jeans, white cotton blouse with a fitted denim waistcoat, and tan riding boots. The jeans hugged her trim figure, and she wore the long sleeves of her blouse rolled up to just below her elbows. Her hair was swept up in a clasp with a few stray wisps dancing around her jawline, while other dark strands clung to the back of her neck.

Now at closer quarters, he could see the clear skin on her face was devoid of makeup and shone with good health, as did the darkly-lashed and luminous brown eyes he'd admired at their first meeting. She had naturally peach-pink cheeks and wore a light gloss on her full lips.

'You look the part too, Maggie.' Dragging his eyes away from her mouth he took a deep breath and squinted at the passing parade.

She too fixed her eyes on the floats, while beneath the soft fabric of her shirt her treacherous heart danced in her chest.

5

As the last floats trundled past, a rowdy bunch of Main Roads staff strolled up to join them, and one of the men nudged Grayson.

'Hey, Reevers, you got a traffic control ticket?'

Grayson nodded.

'Is it current?'

'Yes. Why?'

'The parade marshal's looking for someone to control the traffic while he manoeuvres the floats.' He pointed down the street to where a harassed-looking marshal dashed in and out of log-jammed utes, decorated trailers, horse riders decked out in western gear, school and brass bands, brightly dressed cyclists, and heavy vehicles of all shapes and sizes. 'He asked us to help, but none of us has a current ticket.'

'Right.' With a dip of his hat at Maggie, Grayson strode away.

As she watched him join the marshal, who immediately thumped him on the back and thrust a traffic STOP/GO paddle in his hands, she chewed her lower lip.

There's something about Grayson....

She frowned.

Maybe it's just a bonding thing. Lots of new staff members stick close to me when they first arrive. Although ... that would explain the vibe I'm getting from him, not my reaction to it.

She dropped her gaze and stubbed the toe of her boot against the pavement.

Why am I thinking about stuff like that? I'm a married woman.

But not a happy one.

Damn that defiant inner voice!

She sighed and tried to think about something else. Dwelling on her unhappy marriage didn't change anything and only made her gloomy.

She was given a reprieve when Tom Gilmore shouted, 'Hey, everyone, check out the Not-So-Fat Controller!' and pointed at Grayson, now wearing a high-visibility vest and already in the throes of directing traffic. His height and the brightly coloured vest made him easy to see even for drivers of the larger vehicles.

When Maggie saw the watching marshal give a satisfied nod and scurry off to sort out the jumble of floats, her lips tipped in a proud smile.

. . .

A short while later, with the traffic at last flowing smoothly, the smiling marshal walked up to give Grayson another slap on the back. 'Thanks mate, I owe ya a beer.'

'You're on.' Grayson shrugged out of the vest.

The marshal took it and the paddle from him. 'Right-o, seeya at the pub later.'

When Grayson re-joined the others he was met with a teasing chorus of cheers and applause.

Tom checked his watch and held up a hand to get their attention. 'The sun's over the yardarm now so how about a drink at the pub?' This met with more cheers. 'Okay, let's head to the PO.'

The Post Office Hotel, one of the town's four and a favourite haunt for Main Roads staff, was just around the corner from Maggie and Troy's departmental house. The air had cooled with the setting of the sun so Maggie peeled off, calling, 'I'm popping home for a sec, see you at the pub.'

'Mind if I come with you?'

She gave a start at the sound of Grayson's deep voice right behind her. 'Oh! Um....'

When she looked up at him with a question in her eyes he said quickly, 'It's just that I'm ... curious to see what staff accommodations are like out here. In case at some future time I consider taking up one of those vacant engineering positions you mentioned.'

She grinned. 'Oh, sure. So, do you think that might be a possibility?'

They chatted on the short walk to the house, and when they got there, she wondered idly what her husband's reaction would be to her bringing home 'another' man, especially one like Grayson.

Don't be absurd! Troy isn't bothered by those kinds of things.

She felt a flash of annoyance.

That's because he doesn't regard me as precious. If he did he would've taken the time to know, understand, and love me for who I really am ... but I don't think he has the capacity for that depth of emotion. For him it's all about what he can get from a relationship, nothing more.

Another stab of guilt.

What's got into me?

I've worked hard to come to terms with our less than perfect relationship, and I'm not going to allow old regrets to resurface and spoil that.

With Grayson following close behind she led the way up the stairs. It was only as they neared the top that a sudden thought occurred to her – had the downstairs laundry door been open when they went past? She cringed, picturing the washing she'd pegged out that morning. Had Grayson seen the lacy boy-legs and satin-edged bras hanging pertly on the inside line? Well, it was too late to worry about that now, and she certainly wasn't going to ask him!

She looked over her shoulder as they entered the upper floor and saw him run his eyes over the cream leather lounge strewn with cushions, the patterned floor rugs, Middle Eastern statuettes and wall art, and the decorative but obviously well-equipped kitchen.

'Did the house come furnished, Maggie, or is this your gear?'

'Unfurnished. The interior décor is all mine ... um ... ours.'

He gave an approving nod. 'Nice.'

At a sound from the lounge they turned to see Troy raise his head from where he was sprawled on the three-seater couch. He got to his feet when Maggie introduced Grayson and the men shook hands. Shorter by a good six inches, sporting 'bed' hair from lying on the couch, and wearing his favourite baggy singlet and football shorts, Troy looked stunted and scruffy beside tall, well-dressed Grayson. That didn't appear to bother him, but missing a goal by his football team certainly did. Throwing his hands in the air with an annoyed groan, he sank back onto the couch, eyes once more glued to the screen.

Maggie wondered what impression Grayson would've formed of her husband. He was bound to be a good judge of character, having worked with and supervised a lot of men during his career. Why did Troy have to be so bad-mannered, and make his total lack of interest in anyone other than himself so damn obvious?

She forced a hopeful smile on her face. 'We're all going to the PO for a few drinks, Troy. Wanna come?'

'Nah, don't feel like it.' He yawned, eyes never straying from the TV.

'What about dinner? I was hoping we'd have something to eat at the pub.'

'I'll have last night's leftover spag bols.' He threw the

words over his shoulder, making her feel she was having a conversation with the top of his head.

'You sure?'

'I wouldn't have said it if I wasn't.'

Maggie heard the sliding door onto the patio open and close. Grayson had obviously noticed the acrimonious note in Troy's voice and tactfully removed himself.

Leaning closer to her husband, she said quietly, 'It would be nice if you came along—'

He flicked her a sharp glance. 'Don't start, Maggie.' His gaze returned to the plasma widescreen. 'Go have your fun and leave me in peace to have mine. I've been hanging out to watch this match all day.' He waved a dismissive hand in her direction. 'Seeya when you get home.'

Maggie sighed and headed out to the patio. When Grayson turned at her approach, she glimpsed something like sympathy in his expression. Lifting her chin she said stoutly, 'Well, Troy's not coming so we can go if you like.'

'Right. Say, you've got a nice place here, Maggie.'

With a brisk, 'Thanks,' she spun on her heel and marched back inside to grab her handbag. As she headed to the door with Grayson in tow, she called, 'Seeya, Troy. Not sure what time I'll be home,' and received a grunt in reply.

Grayson got no acknowledgement from him at all.

Maggie was silent on the walk to the pub. She felt deflated, as was always the case after a run-in with Troy. Grayson seemed happy to stroll by her side without speaking, every now and then looking up to take in the stars filling the evening sky. She could have hugged him for being so considerate.

When they reached the pub, they found the others seated at a large table and a few of the blokes leaning on the bar. More townsfolk stood or sat in groups, laughing and chatting and nodding at new arrivals whether they knew them or not. Country music pumped from a battered juke box in the softly lit bar room, and delicious aromas of grilling steak and garlic hung in the air.

Grayson touched her arm. 'I'll get our drinks. What'll you have?'

'A glass of sauv blanc, thanks. My shout for the next round, right?'

He nodded and watched her join the Main Roads table, before making his way through the crowd to the bar. When Tom sidled up beside him, Grayson dipped his head in greeting.

Leaning his back against the bar so he could survey the room, Tom said coolly, 'So ... you went to Maggie's place?' His carefully nonchalant tone had Grayson's eyes creasing at the corners.

When the barmaid set a glass of beer dripping with condensation in front of him, Grayson picked it up in one large hand and smiled at Tom over the head of froth. 'Yes, I did. Wanted to see what the accommodations are like in this part of the world ... in case I decide to move up here one day, you know?'

With a shrewd, 'Yeah, I think I do know,' Tom raised an eyebrow at him.

Grayson gave an amused snort and clinked his glass against Tom's, before taking a long swig of beer. He swallowed and breathed, 'Ah, that's good. You Aussies sure know how to brew a good lager.'

Tom grinned. 'Well, thanks very much. And you Poms sure know how to drink it.'

Their laughter drew the attention of the others at the bar, and they were soon surrounded by a large group.

Maggie glanced over at them and sighed. Conversation ... something she could rarely enjoy at home where cut-to-the-chase exchanges were the norm. Troy wasn't interested in 'frivolous' discussions about things like dreams or reminiscences, and walked out on her attempts to start them. It wasn't always because he was angry, he simply wasn't interested in hearing what she had to say. Taking a deep breath, she lifted her chin and rose to join the noisy group.

Grayson had another frothing schooner in his hand and two more lined up on the bar in front of him, courtesy of the parade marshal making good on his promise, and was amusing the group with tales of engineering, sporting, and partying feats in the UK. Maggie took the opportunity to study his strong facial features, but when her eyes travelled down to admire his broad chest and well-defined, muscular arms, she hastily looked away. Taking a sip of wine, she closed her eyes and let the rich velvet of his deep voice envelop her. She could listen to it all day....

'Maggie!'

Her eyes snapped open. Tom stood in front of her, and everyone else was looking at her.

Heat radiated up her neck and into her cheeks. 'Oh! Sorry, what?'

A grinning Tom nudged her. 'Where were you?'

'Just ... daydreaming. Did I miss something?'

'We were talking about the things we'll remember most about the Curry when we leave, and Reevers asked you what yours would be ... twice.'

'Sorry, I ... didn't hear....' She cleared her throat. 'The thing I'll most remember? Well....' She could tell they expected a funny story but her brain was switching between total paralysis one moment and grasshopper leaps the next. And then she remembered her first run-in with a gidgee bug.

It would have to do.

Gathering her wits, she turned to Grayson with a boldness she didn't feel. 'Have you heard of the famous gidgee bug?' As soon as she said it, versions of, 'Oh yeah, the damn gidgee bugs....' did the rounds.

Grayson shook his head. 'Not the bug, no. Only the gidgee weed.'

'Ooh, that bloody stink weed,' a voice moaned.

'Well,' Maggie went on, 'gidgee bugs are annual visitors to town, perhaps more aptly described as invaders,' at which the group as one gave loud groans. 'They're big, shiny, almost iridescent and arrive around Christmas time, so you'd be forgiven for confusing them with everyone's favourite, the Christmas beetle. At the height of the season the office floor is thick with them, so they're hard to avoid.'

There were murmurs of, 'Yep, that's right,' and, 'Just thick with 'em.'

'My first run-in with these ... shall we say ... *colourful* little critters,' which produced a round of sniggers, 'was when I accidentally squashed one under the wheels of my office chair.' Maggie paused to let the cries of 'Oh no!' and 'Eeoo!' to fade before continuing. 'After which I was forced to endure the incredible stench its death throes produced – which, by the way, lingered long after the corpse was disposed of.'

There was a ripple of empathetic discomfort through the audience, making Grayson conclude that gidgee bug squashing was a shared experience among the townsfolk.

Maggie raised her voice again. 'Then came the complaints from my esteemed colleagues,' and she paused for chuckles and, 'Here-here's,' from the audience, 'who shared what was then an open plan office.'

Another voice piped up. 'Yeah, I was one of them. That damn bug was the worst I've ever smelt, and I've squished a few in my time. Brought bloody tears to my eyes!'

This met with loud laughter as Maggie carried on. 'Yes, well like Peta here, everyone held their noses, looks of sick anguish on their faces while darting barbed glances in my direction.' Her exaggerated expressions and gestures had everyone chortling. 'So by the time the regional director, who was still new to Cloncurry back then, came into the office,' and she once more directed her words at Grayson, 'I was well and truly flustered. And when he asked, "What's that awful smell?", naturally I said, "Oh, sorry Harry, it was me".'

By this time the group was in stitches, and when one of them leaped forward to imitate the regional director's shocked expression, Maggie had to wait for the hilarity to subside before bringing the story to a close.

'And the moral of this tale?' she said over the top of the noise, prompting a relative hush. 'Well, my advice to you, Grayson, and to all our newbies is ... if you want to succeed in the Curry, stay alert to what's crawling under your chair,' to which the crowd as one gave a soft, drawn-out 'woooh'.

'... avoid getting personal with a gidgee bug if you possibly can,' and the crowd hooted.

'... and, most importantly, never claim a bad smell as your own,' which once more filled the room with uproarious noise.

There was a burst of applause and a voice yelled, 'Yeah Reevers, so if y'gonna get personal with someone, make it someone your own size – if you can find one that is!' and everyone laughed again.

Still smiling, Maggie resumed her seat at the table. As she leaned down to take a tissue from her handbag, a pair of dusty work boots appeared in her line of vision. She looked up to see Grayson grinning down at her.

'That was a good story, and you're a natural story teller.'

She smiled her thanks. 'As are you, judging by your growing fan club.'

They glanced at the gradually dispersing group at the bar.

'I think you'll find they just like a bit of new blood, and hearing about how the other half lives.' He indicated the seat beside her. 'May I?'

'Be my guest, although you might want to make sure

there aren't any gidgee bugs under there, waiting to be squished.'

He chuckled and eased his long frame into the chair. She tried to make room for him but the table had become quite crowded. Proximity to him was ... what? Unsettling? Pleasing? Both? She couldn't decide.

When he leaned across to speak to the person on the other side of her she noticed a hint of ruddiness beneath the tanned skin of his face, courtesy of the numerous beers bought for him by all and sundry no doubt. Except for the emerging dark stubble on his jawline, his face and neck were smooth and very ... touchable.

When he turned and caught her staring she spluttered, 'Must be my shout for the drinks.' Not that he needed more alcohol by the looks of things, but she couldn't think of a better reason to excuse herself.

He gazed into her eyes and said with only a slight slur, 'Another beer would be great, ta.'

She pushed her chair back, relieved to escape the warm, electrified fog that had somehow enveloped them, and headed to the even more crowded bar. When she finally returned to the table, Grayson stood to take the beer glass from her, with a surprisingly steady hand.

Their fingers touched and lingered for an instant, firm warm skin against soft warm skin, until she recoiled as though zapped by two-forty volts. He reacted too, sucking in a breath and raking darkening eyes over her face before his gaze settled on her open lips. At the sensual intimacy in that gaze she covered her mouth with a hand and stared back at him with wide, shocked eyes. As if jarred by the realisation they'd somehow crossed the line between friendly mateship and man-woman awareness, he frowned and took a step back.

Maggie felt like a possum stunned into immobility by bright headlights. Dropping her hand to her side she took a ragged breath. When her flustered, 'Um....' came out in a squeak, she hastily shut her mouth again.

Grayson's voice too was uneven when he rasped, 'Maggie,' and reached out a hand, but she was already moving away, pushing through the crowd. He swore under his breath and bent his head to scowl at the dusty wooden floor. When he looked up again, there was no sign of her in the room. After casually making his way to the door he saw her walking homeward, and watched until she disappeared into the darkness. Leaning on the door jamb, he bumped his head against the wood a couple of times.

What the hell was he doing, coming on to someone else's wife?

Not for all the money in the world would he inflict pain like that on another man.

Turning on his heel he headed back to the bar, where he gave the metal footrest a satisfying kick before resting his forearms on the beer-soaked bar runner. Too many beers had already got him in trouble so he ordered a soda water instead, hoping it might quench at least one of the thirsts he'd developed.

6

The rodeo crowd was at its peak early in the bright, cloudless day. Numbers would drop significantly in the searing midday heat, to rally again in the relative cool of the afternoon.

Grayson stood at the timber fence surrounding the cattle yards with Tom and Lisa Gilmore. With one work-booted foot resting on the bottom rail, he squinted through the dust cloud at the calf-roping event. While they hadn't been there long, already a gritty red layer of dust coated not only their boots but their jeans, shirts, and wide-brimmed hats as well, something the Gilmores appeared to take in their stride. Their two children had deserted the adults in favour of running around with their friends, like a mob of brumby colts.

Grayson uncrossed his arms from along the top rail and straightened to sweep another glance around the crowd.

Tom nudged him with an elbow. 'You lookin' for someone?'

'No ... well, not really.' Grayson glanced at him sideways. 'I don't know all that many people here yet.'

Tom was about to say something more when Lisa put a hand on his arm.

'Hey hon, I'm going to check on the kids, make sure they're not up to any mischief.'

He nodded and she hurried away. Turning back, he found Grayson once more engrossed in the frenzied tussle between man and beast. The cut and thrust of hooves and heels in the yard created more dust clouds that rose into the already russet haze above the rodeo ground.

Tom leaned against the fence and drawled, 'Reckon I can guess. You're lookin' for Maggie, right?'

A tight-lipped Grayson eyed the calf now on the ground, flailing its legs as the sweating, red-faced roper strove to hog-tie it.

Tom gave an amused grunt. 'Hey, don't feel embarrassed, Reevers. Maggie's a great girl, and fun to be around. But you haven't forgotten she's married, right?'

'Of course not.' Grayson continued gazing straight ahead.

'Okay, well as long as all you're doin' is lookin' and not hurtin' anyone, what's the harm?' Tom slapped him on the shoulder. 'Now, the next competitor's a local boy and should be in with a good chance.'

Ringside spectator numbers swelled as the rough-and-tumble action began again. The dust thickened, hanging lower all the time, and as more competitors battled to win the substantial prize money, the temperature rose ... and rose some more. Grayson was glad when the thirsty Gilmore children gave him a reason to buy cold drinks all round, and take a break from the billowing dust and heat of the crowd. As he ambled to the drinks van he glimpsed familiar faces in a group standing near the bar. One of them was Troy Kerr. He was looking around with an expression of abject boredom. There was a dark, glossy head beside him.

As Grayson drew near, Troy stared through him without any hint of recognition, until Grayson walked up to him, hand extended. 'G'day mate.' They shook hands and then Grayson lifted his hat to run a hand over his head, adding another recently learned Aussieism, 'It's a warm one, alright.'

'Yep.' Troy turned away, clearly uninterested in further conversation.

The snub was lost on Grayson. He was already gazing at Maggie, who'd whirled around on hearing his deep voice. He saw a look of uncertainty cross her features as she gave him a nod in greeting, and then turned back to the others.

Once more silently berating himself for having tipsily overstepped the mark the evening before, he decided to avoid the bar tent despite his yearning for a cold beer. And then he heard one of the engineers in the group say cheerily, 'Hey, Reevers is here.' His expression lifted as most in the group looked his way with welcoming grins.

'Hello chaps, Having a good time are we?'

'Sure are,' the cheery man replied. 'Hey, we're looking for more willing bodies to enter the corporate novelty races – you in? We just *gotta* beat Ergon Energy this year. They've done us over twice in two years now! We can't let that happen again.'

Feeling all eyes on him, including Maggie's, he answered more quickly than he might otherwise have done. 'I'm up for it.'

This met with cheers and back-thumping, and then the cheery man grabbed him by the arm. 'C'mon, we gotta register our team.'

'Alright, but first I have to buy some drinks.'

As the group dispersed, Troy grabbed Maggie's arm. 'I'm going to the bar.' He inclined his head toward the noisy throng in the bar tent.

'But Troy, the fun's just starting—' She winced as his fingers bit into the soft flesh of her upper arm. He didn't seem to notice. Releasing his hold, he walked off with a spring in his step. As Maggie stood rubbing her arm, unsure whether to feel deserted or delighted, she saw him greet his beer-swilling mates with fist bumps, name-calling and coarse laughter.

Turning on her heel, she hurried after the happy Main Roads group.

On their way to the competition tent Grayson stopped at the refreshments van and then sought out the dusty, sweating, and by now parched Gilmores. While handing out the icy-cold cans of softdrink, which were immediately opened and their chilled contents consumed, he announced, 'Well, I've been roped into competing in the novelty races. Am I going to regret this?'

Tom and Lisa both laughed and Tom spluttered, 'Nothing surer!'

Grayson gave an exaggerated groan, just as the cheery man's eyes alighted on Tom.

'Hey Tom, we need another person for the three-legged race – someone tall enough to go with Reevers. We were going to put him with Chandra, but ... there's a bit of a size difference.'

The understatement raised a group chuckle.

Lisa nudged her husband. 'Go on, you'll have fun and so will I, watching you make a clown of yourself.'

'Oh, alright then.' Amid the group cheer Tom raised his voice. 'But don't expect too much, I'm no champion tripedal y'know!' He walked up to stand beside Grayson. 'Alright big fella, our honour's on the line here. We need to win this by hook or by crook.'

To the loud whistles and catcalls from the growing number of spectators for the three-legged race heats, the first Main Roads competitors stepped up to the starting line. Another late conscript, engineer Suman was a close match to Chandra in height. They did well in their race, leaving the Ergon Energy team for dead to rousing applause and cheers from their co-workers. Grayson and Tom watched from the sideline, taking note of the most successful techniques. And then it was their turn.

Watching from where she stood at the back of the crowd, Maggie couldn't help smiling as the two men launched themselves from the starting post and charged down the course with their inside legs firmly tied together. Clumsy at first, they grew more confident as Grayson matched his longer stride to Tom's, and they gained momentum.

Having won that heat they joined Chandra and Suman in the next race, the egg-and-spoon, where competitors had to balance egg-laden spoons in their mouths and run to the finish line without dropping their fragile cargo. When the four of them were successful in completing that challenge, they had to compete against each other in the sack race to determine overall individual champion.

Trackside, the Main Roads group was like an over-excited flock of noisy mina birds, squawking, cheering, and calling out good-natured ribbing at the defeated Ergon Energy team. Grayson looked on in amusement while he stood waiting for the sack race to begin, and noticed a youngish woman in the group, dressed in a brightly coloured sari. She looked exotic and out of place among all the jeans and checked shirts, and he wondered if she might be Chandra's wife. When he saw the little man give her a shy wave, he knew he'd guessed right.

Sweeping his gaze over the crowd, his eyes found Maggie's. This time there was no sign of Troy. Grayson was pleased to see a mixture of pride and amusement in Maggie's expression, and when she smiled at him he beamed back, glad he'd decided to curtail his beer intake.

Maybe it was time he reined in the drinking habit he'd

formed since parting with Tina? It was social drinking more than anything, and helped keep the loneliness and painful memories at bay. It could also get him in trouble if he wasn't careful....

Dragging his eyes from Maggie's face, he made himself concentrate on the race. As in every competition, he played to win.

At the starter's shout, 'Don your sacks!' the competitors scrambled to pull up the scratchy hessian bags over their knees. As the starter's pistol rang out they all took off, stumbling and kangaroo-jumping their way down the track. This time Grayson's height proved a disadvantage. After struggling to get the sack up to a workable level, he finally left the starting line with Tom, Chandra, and Suman all ahead of him in the field.

Not for long.

Maggie held her breath as she watched Grayson settle into the movement and begin to gather speed. The muscles in his arms bulged as he gripped the top edge of the sack to keep it from bunching around his feet. He wore a determined expression until he caught up with the others, when his lips broke into a wide grin.

By this time the competitors' wives and families were all yelling encouragement. Caught up in the excitement, and as the four competitors neared the finish line in a huddle with Grayson nudging the front, Maggie jumped up and down, shouting, 'Go Grayson, go!' Together with the calls of, 'Go Chandra!', 'Go Suman!', 'Go Tom!', it made for a fine, rousing chant.

And then the calls turned into a communal, dismayed gasp when Grayson lost his footing and tumbled to the ground close to the finish line, his legs a hessian-wrapped tangle when he hit the dirt. Rolling onto his stomach, he lifted his head in time to see Chandra take a final winning leap over the line, followed closely by Tom and Suman, to a loud chorus of cheers.

Maggie found herself in the crush of wives and families running onto the track to congratulate the competitors. She slowed to approach Grayson with what she hoped was a casual air.

Just to check he's alright.

He had tossed the sack to one side and was sitting on the ground, one long leg stretched in front of him and the other bent, an arm slung over it. With his other hand he shaded his eyes while gazing toward the finish line, where Chandra was doing a victorious Rocky impersonation. Maggie noticed he was grinning.

Grinning at having lost?

She knelt beside him on the grass. 'Are you okay?'

'Oh sure, I'm fine.'

'That was some tumble you took.'

'Did it look as impressive as it felt?' He pulled a face and pretended to gingerly rub the back of his neck.

'Oh yes, very impressive.'

They shared a smile as Tom came over to give Grayson a hand up. Putting on a bad pommy accent he said, 'Downright sportsmanlike of you, old man.'

Maggie stared at him. Sportsmanlike? What was Tom talking about?

Grayson threw her a sheepish glance as Tom went on. 'You would've blitzed it if you hadn't chucked it in at the end. But hey, it worked!' At Grayson's quick frown, Tom added with a grin, 'Yeah, I know what you did, and why you did it.' He lifted his chin to indicate the cheering crowd gathered around Chandra, who only had eyes for his sari-clad wife. She stood in front of him smiling proudly. And then the crowd closed in around them and they were lost in the mêlée of vigorous hand-shaking and back-slapping.

Tom turned back to Grayson. 'You struck me as a some-what serious competitor, Reevers me old mate, so that was – how would you say it? – *jolly decent* of you.'

Maggie gazed wide-eyed at Grayson. 'Did you fall on purpose so Chandra could be a winner in front of his new wife?'

Grayson opened his mouth to confess only to pause when he spotted the lady in question coming to stand within earshot. She had moved out of the way when the crowd lifted her husband into the air to a loud, out-of-tune chorus of 'We are the champions'. With a significant glance at Tom and Maggie, Grayson said loud enough for Chandra's wife to hear, 'No, the better man won, hands down.'

They turned to see her looking first at Grayson's impres-sive form and then at her little husband – a man she barely knew, chosen for her by her family in the Nepalese tradition – with a glow of pride and love on her face.

Tom gave Grayson a resounding slap on his broad back. 'You're alright, y'know Reevers. For a bloody Pom.'

'And in the first race on today's programme, we have a number of locally bred and trained thoroughbreds....' The announcer's nasal voice over the loudspeaker was barely audible above the din of the betting arena.

It was the first race day of the season, and the whole town – and every sticky black fly in existence, it seemed – had turned out for it. As usual, the townsfolk embraced the opportunity to don glad rags and to dress their children in smart Western attire and miniature Akubras. As soon as the youngsters lined up for the first lolly drop from the high steward's box, however, all thoughts of staying clean were gone in the scramble to collect as many sweets as possible from where they fell on the prickly ground.

Maggie gave up trying to hear the announcements and wandered over to look at the bookies' boards and compare the odds offered for her chosen horse. When the nearest bookie glanced at her, she held out a ten dollar note. 'Our Blue Boy in race one, for a win, thanks.'

'Are you sure?' a voice at her elbow said. 'He's got big odds which means he's a roughie.'

She turned to see Tom standing beside her, gazing at the board. 'You know me, Tom, I've got a soft spot for roughies.' She glanced over his shoulder and saw Lisa give a smiling wave from where she stood chatting with friends. Maggie returned the smile and the wave, glad as always to have their company so she didn't feel out of place being there on her own.

After going out of their way to befriend her when she first arrived in Cloncurry, as though realising how alone she felt in the world, the Gilmores had become her closest friends, second only to Evie.

Tom flicked a glance over her outfit. 'You're lookin' mighty fine today, missus, if I may say so.'

She gave an exaggerated flutter of long, dark eyelashes while raising a hand to check her delicate pink and cream fascinator was still in place. She'd chosen to wear her hair loose, and it fell in glossy waves past her carefully made-up face, to where the off-the shoulder sleeves of her salmon-pink cocktail dress revealed the satiny quality of her skin. The dress's fitted bodice hugged her trim figure and tapered to a narrow waistline above the knee-length skirt, beneath which her tanned legs were smooth and bare above high-heeled cream court shoes. 'And I could say the same about you and Lisa.'

'But we don't make quite the waves that you do, my dear.' He grinned at her, and they both looked over to where a number of openly admiring men was gathering. 'As usual, the moths are attracted to your flame.'

At the impish twinkle in his eyes she said drily, 'Oh come on, Tom. They're just the guys from work. But thanks for the compliment.'

He grinned and then sobered. 'Troy not with you?'

'No, he's working this week.'

'Oh, what a shame.'

'Being sarcastic doesn't suit you, Tom.'

At her lift of a mock-disapproving eyebrow, he gave a bark of laughter. 'I'm glad we've been friends long enough to enjoy each other's honesty.'

She grinned. 'True.'

Lisa sashayed up to join them as Tom spied Grayson making his way through the crowd.

Mumbling, ''Scuse me ladies,' he headed over to welcome him with a clap on the shoulder and a robust greeting.

A smiling Lisa turned to Maggie. 'Tom likes him, you know, that new bloke. Reckons he's alright.'

As the men strode up to them Grayson eyed the two women with open admiration. 'Hello ladies. My, don't you look scrumptious.' This earned him coy smiles, while Tom rolled his eyes.

'Enough of the sweet-talk, mate. How about we get some drinks going?'

'Right you are.'

As the men headed to the bar, Maggie took in the way Grayson's fitted black jeans hugged his powerful build. He'd rolled up the long sleeves of his western-style checked shirt to the elbows, revealing well-defined forearms. Glancing down, she noted the dull shine on his work boots, and realised he must've made an effort to polish them. A smile tugged at her lips. He'd certainly gone to some trouble for the occasion. She glanced around the crowd and couldn't find a more manly-looking specimen, even among the construction workers and farmers.

'Yeah,' a clearly amused Lisa said in her ear, 'not bad at all.'

Maggie was about to protest when a piercing shriek emanated from the loud speaker above their heads, and the crackly announcer's voice emerged above the din. 'Ladies and gents, sorry about this. There'll be a slight delay to the start of the first race. The jockey club representative has inspected the course and pronounced it unsatisfactory. So we'll have to wait until someone wakes up Bluey so he can give the course another quick going over with his grader.'

Then, when nothing happened, 'Bluey? You here? Anyone seen Bluey?'

There was movement in the crowd and a portly, red-faced man emerged from the bar area, still clutching a stubby of beer.

'Orright, orright! I 'erd yez the first time.' Amid the chuckles, Bluey made his unsteady way to a faded yellow grader parked behind the stables.

A voice rose from the crowd in a sing-song recitation. 'Nothing in a hurry when you're living in the Curry,' which met with amused murmurs. Nobody appeared overly surprised or perturbed by the delay, nor were there any obvious concerns about Bluey's fitness to operate the grader, despite the clues he might be somewhat 'under the weather'. It was probably thought he couldn't do much damage just driving it slowly around a clearly-defined track.

When the two men returned from the bar, drinks in

hand, Grayson gave Maggie a cold glass of bubbly and Tom passed one to Lisa. Maggie thanked him but felt a pinch of concern. Did the four of them – she, Grayson, Tom and Lisa – look like two couples?

She bit her lip.

It was very easy for small town people to get the wrong idea about things like that.

Had it occurred to Grayson some folk might draw that conclusion?

When she glanced up at him, she found him looking as proud as Punch standing there beside her, so he probably wouldn't care what people thought.

Easy for him, he's not married.

The speaker shrilled again and the announcer's voice once more cut through the din. 'Ladies and gentlemen, the first race will be commencing soon, thanks to the efforts of our mate, Bluey.' All eyes turned to see the grader slowly trundling onto the track. 'And in the saddling enclosure, the fine steeds competing in the first race are being paraded for your perusal. Please come and toast some excellent examples of horse flesh.'

Seizing the opportunity to extract herself from the 'cosy couples' scene, Maggie said crisply, 'Great, I want to see what my horse looks like.' Dropping her clutch purse on the table, she hurried to the fence surrounding the enclosure. Just as she got there Bluey decided he was in the right spot to begin grading, and lowered the blade. In his beery fog, he misjudged the position, and when the blade dug into a previously ungraded surface, a dense cloud of dust and dried grass rose into the air. It was immediately caught by the warm breeze and blown straight over the saddling enclosure.

Tom, Lisa and Grayson stopped on their way to the fence when Maggie turned toward them with arms raised, dismay and disbelief on her now grimy face. Red dust and dried grass now coated her from her once shiny hair to her patent leather shoes. And when she took off her dust-caked sunglasses, the circles of clean skin around her eyes made her look like a russet-n-white minstrel.

After a moment of shocked silence, Tom blustered, 'Wow girl, you're covered in a whole lot of Australia!' and suddenly everyone was laughing, even the casualty herself.

Gaping in amazement at her, Grayson could only manage a choked, 'Oh...,' while trying not to laugh.

'Yeah, "oh" is right.' Tom chortled. 'Welcome to Cloncurry, where you never know when you're going to be covered in sh—'

'Tom!' Lisa scolded, 'spare a thought for poor Maggie.'

'Oh yeah ... sorry, Maggie love,' he said, trying to keep the amusement out of his voice. 'What can we do to fix you up?'

She threw him a rueful grin and glanced down at her dust and grass-covered dress, just as Lisa took her to one side and began brushing her down.

Beside Tom, Grayson said quietly, 'She took that well, considering. Another woman – my ex for example – would've been bawling by now.'

''Course she took it well.' The pride was obvious in Tom's voice. 'That's our Maggie for ya. She's a *real* person, not some prima donna who goes to pieces when she breaks a finger-nail ... or gets semi-buried in outback dust.'

Grayson nodded thoughtfully and watched Lisa continue with her ministrations.

As Maggie stood with her arms raised, her eyes alighted on something Grayson was holding. It was pink ... and shiny ... her clutch purse! What the—? And then she noticed the two cameras slung around his neck. Hang on.... She looked back at their table near the betting arena. It was empty.

He'd brought everyone's valuables with him.

'That's about the best I can do, I'm afraid.' Lisa gave her skirt one more pat and stood back.

Maggie glanced down at herself and then gave her friend a grateful smile. 'Thanks, that's a lot better.'

The two women made their way to where Tom and Grayson stood idly chatting. Before Maggie could say anything about the purse and cameras, Grayson fixed her with a sympathetic gaze and said, 'What a thing to happen, love. I hope your dress will be alright.'

Love.

He'd called her love.

The word bounced around inside her, leaving sweet sugar stings wherever it hit.

Hang on, isn't 'love' a common British idiom? And hadn't Tom called her that without sending her emotions into a frenzy?

'Thanks. I'm sure it'll be fine, it's only dust.' She pointed to the gear he was carrying. 'Hey, why did you bring all that with you?'

'What?' He glanced down at it. 'Oh … well, we were all going to the fence. Nobody was staying behind to keep an eye on it.'

'It was perfectly fine on the table. No one would've touched it there.'

His expression grew sheepish. 'I lived in Glasgow for a while, you see. There, if you turn your back on something remotely valuable, it would be gone by the time you turned 'round again. I lost a treasured ham sandwich that way once.' His eyes twinkled. 'Old habits die hard.'

She gave a tinkling laugh. 'Oh, well then, I guess thanks are in order.' When she indicated her purse he handed it to her. 'I *am* rather fond of this particular ham sandwich.' They laughed together and she added, 'I'm glad Cloncurry isn't Glasgow, and our valuables are quite safe when we leave them unattended for a bit.' With a smiling nod at him, she headed ringside again to watch the horses lining up at the barrier.

As his eyes followed her, Grayson's thoughts turned to Troy Kerr. How could he risk leaving something as valuable as her 'unattended'? It just wasn't safe....

7

Harry put his head around the doorway to her office. 'I've decided on this year's Unity Day comp.'

Maggie's shoulders slumped. That time of year already? Surely it was only a few months since she'd organised the last 'warm-n-fuzzy' Unity Day? Every state office was expected – directed – to hold team-building activities that day to foster closer working relationships, and in Cloncurry that usually meant some sort of competition between the white collar Corporate and blue collar Commercial sectors.

'A lawn bowls competition,' Harry went on sounding pleased with himself, 'between us and the commercial boys, naturally.' He flashed her a winning smile. 'Can I leave it with you to organise?' At her lukewarm expression, he coaxed, 'Samantha can give you a hand. C'mon, it'll be fun.'

Fun for participants, sure, just more work for the organisers.

'Okay.' She sighed. 'You're the boss.'

'Great. I'll get Samantha to locate the trophy.'

Maggie nodded and wondered idly whether the revered if crudely made Unity Day trophy had survived another year.

Maggie was partway through writing another team name when the chalk slipped from her grip and she scraped a fingernail down the wall-mounted blackboard. Wincing, she climbed down the stepladder to retrieve the chalk from off the floor.

It would've been handy to have Troy there to help with the competition preparations, but he'd declined without bothering to make an excuse. And if she were honest, it was a relief to be free of his company, even if that meant one less helping hand.

She climbed the ladder again, her thoughts on last evening. After eating dinner in virtual silence, they had settled in the lounge to watch TV with barely a word passing between them. That had become the norm for their evenings together. Troy was happy with that, it was his idea of companionship.

It wasn't hers.

The evenings she'd spent at home with her parents were so very different. They would often turn off the idiot box to talk, share their thoughts, ideas, and memories. Her heart swelled with longing. Why couldn't she and Troy make that sort of connection? They were both adults, surely they could build an intellectual compatibility if they tried hard enough? But her attempts to engage her husband in conversation always ended in disappointment. At best, his replies were monosyllabic. At worst, he ignored her and turned up the volume on the TV, or asked her to be quiet. It seemed bullet-point exchanges on the mechanics of their daily lives was her lot now.

She gave a resigned sigh.

At least she had Evie at the end of the phone or email when she needed to talk about something other than the latest bank statement or electricity bill.

'Hey Mags, whatcha doin'?'

She gave a start, forced a smile, and turned to greet a group of her workmates. 'Glad you're here guys, I could use a hand.' She was greeted with silence, broken only by chuckles as the others scanned the names she'd written on the board.

One of the men read them aloud. 'Works Manager Jim "Just-Roll-The-Damn-Thing" Jackson, Regional Director "Hard-ball" Harry Cochrane, Engineers "Bowlarama Bob Evans" and "Rock-n-Roll-it Robert Ramsay", and "Tom The-Bowling-Great Gilmore".'

A voice rose above the mirth. 'Hey Maggie, I don't see your name up there, or Grayson's?'

'I haven't thought up any for us yet.'

'What about "Make-out Maggie" and "Go-get-'er Grayson"?' one wag suggested with a snicker.

She eyed the speaker and said firmly, 'It's *supposed* to be bowls-related, Bob.'

Everyone sniggered and Bob pretended to look contrite. 'Just kidding.'

Another voice piped up. 'Hey, how about "Marvellous Maggie"?'

'Nah, too boring!' someone else said.

Smiling at their enthusiasm, Maggie went back to writing on the board while the discussion carried on behind her.

'Magic Maggie?'

'Sounds too much like Monkey Magic!'

'Ahhh, Monkeee. Ahhh, Pigzeee!' There was a group guffaw.

'C'mon guys, we gotta think of some good ones.'

'How about "More-ish Maggie"?'

'What's that supposed to mean?'

'You know, she's more-ish – a good sort.'

'Yeah, well we all know that. But what's it got to do with bowls?'

'Well....'

'I know!' Bob exclaimed, 'What about "Mow-em-down-Maggie"?'

'Hey yeah, that's not bad! What do you think, Maggie?'

'Sorry, what?' She tuned into the conversation again.

'We've come up with a name for you, "Mow-em-down Maggie". What d'ya think?'

Tilting her head to the side and crinkling her chin, she mused aloud, 'Mm ... not bad. Thanks guys, I think I'll go with it.' Turning, she promptly added it to the growing list of competitors' names on the board.

Samantha raised a hand as if in school. 'And what about "Go-go Grayson"?'

'Or "Grab-n-go Grayson",' another of the women crooned.

'Come on, Peta,' Bob taunted, 'just 'cos you wish he'd grab *you* 'n go....'

There were more sniggers.

'You're gettin' denser in your old age, Bob Evans.' Peta punched him on the arm. 'For your information, I meant grab a *bowl*-n-go. And I'll have you know I haven't got the hots for anyone 'cept my Roger.' She smothered a girlish giggle.

Samantha piped up again. 'Alright then, what about "Gorgeous Grayson"?'

Peta nodded. 'Yeah, suits him. Not that he's *gorgeous*, just sort of hunky in a *mmm MMM* sorta way—'

'Okay!' The discussion had gone far enough for Maggie. '"Go-go Grayson" it is.'

This met with exclamations of, 'Woohoo! Two outta two, how good are we!'

Maggie grinned. 'Now, how about you guys help set up the kitchen for the sausage sizzle?'

'Right you are.' Bob rubbed his hands together. 'We'll get busy soon as we've wet our whistles.' They headed to the bar. Once out of earshot he whispered to the group, 'Mow-em-down Maggie is right! I've caught Go-go Grayson lookin' at her like he wishes he was the lawn and she was the mower.'

Peta rolled her eyes and glowered at him as one of the others exclaimed, 'Oh Bob, *again* with the mower thing, you're obsessed!' Everyone laughed and even the busy bartender, being thrown orders from all along the bar, gave a loud chortle.

Later that day, Grayson walked to the lawn bowls club. The cap lent him by one of the other engineers and embroidered with the words, *Go Ahead, Bowl Me Over,* gave some protection from the sun, but by the time he got near the clubhouse he was hot, sweating, and thirsty.

Inside, Peta spied him approaching and rushed to the window. She stood, doe-eyed, taking in his long legs in well-worn blue jeans and the snug fit of his red polo shirt over firm chest muscles and biceps, and let out a hot breath.

Unaware he was being watched, Grayson strode along the blistering pavement anticipating a cold drink and a fun time. Social occasions like this bowls comp would be important for the wellbeing of remote area residents, he decided. Would *he* be able to stand the isolation long-term?

Probably not.

He wouldn't even choose to live alone unless, like now, it was forced on him. Lifting his cap, he ran an agitated hand over his head.

At least in the city, surrounded by people, he'd made friends easily enough. It was a different ballgame in a place like Cloncurry, though.... According to Tom, most of the town's residents were public servants on remote service, so at Christmas time everyone went home for the holidays, leaving the deserted town in 'stand-by' mode.

Home for Grayson was too far away to return every year, despite his mother's pleading. So if he lived in Cloncurry, he'd either be a 'Christmas orphan' if lucky enough to join another family for the festivities, or just plain lonely. He sighed. He didn't 'do' lonely well – it gave him too much time to think. Safer to stay active and fall into bed at night, too tired to dwell on past mistakes.

Striding to the clubhouse's door, he pushed it open and stepped into the building's artificial coolness, to be greeted by the smell of spilt beer and musty carpet. People stood three deep waiting to catch the eye of the barman, who was busily filling multiple schooners for his thirsty customers. Amid the din of voices, Grayson's ears caught occasional snatches of country music.

He swept a glance around the crowded room and spotted one team who'd dressed for the occasion in oversized sombreros, grass skirts and Hawaiian shirts. He grinned. It was obvious everyone was there for a good time.

Behind them Tom raised an hand and called, 'Reevers! We're over here!' He was standing in a group of Main Roads engineers.

After making his way through the throng Grayson said, 'Afternoon, chaps. Everyone ready for some fierce competition with those commercial cowboys?'

'You bet, Go-go!' several voices chimed.

Tom shook Grayson's hand. 'Glad to see you made it, mate. Can I shout you a beer?'

'Cheers. I'll come with you.' They sauntered to the bar. 'Say, did I hear right? They just called me "Go-go"?'

'Yep. "Go-go Grayson" is your bowling name.' Tom indicated the blackboard and then glanced sideways at him. 'And you can stop looking, she's not here yet.'

'I'm just checking out the opposition is all.'

'Well, if that's true, I'm betting you've come to the same conclusion I have.'

'Which is?'

'That we've got this game in the bag!' Tom gave Grayson's arm a playful punch as the barman approached to take their order.

While they waited for their drinks, Grayson read the names on the blackboard and nudged Tom with an elbow. 'Maybe I should be shouting *you* a drink, "Tom the Great".'

Out on the green the setting sun created long shadows across the lawn, and the soft, warm breeze fanned the mix of experienced, novice, and first-time-lucky bowlers. Spectators enjoyed the combination of skilful rolls and explosive off-the-end-gutter shots. At the historic Wagon Wheel restaurant next door most diners had chosen to eat out on the deck, from there they could watch the action and call out encouragement or good-natured ribbing.

The restaurant's owners had, a little optimistically perhaps, planted palm trees in the garden area that bordered the bowling green. The trees had grown surprisingly well, despite the dry climate, and now their gently swaying silhouettes against the sunset served as reminders of the town's tropical north-west location, in a state that regarded Cloncurry as its 'warm heart'.

Dressed for comfort in a sleeveless cotton blouse and khaki cargo pants, Maggie stood on the edge of the green, scrunching her toes into the grass and thankful this was a barefoot competition. She watched Tom lead the Crushers team to victory over the Cowboys. Maggie's team, the Champs, also beat their opponents, the Crocodiles.

Later, everyone gathered in the clubhouse for the trophy presentation. Maggie made her way to where Lisa Gilmore stood with Tom and Grayson, chatting over cold glasses of beer. When Grayson offered to buy her a drink Maggie accepted. She'd already had one but didn't have to worry about being over the limit. Home was only a short walk away.

'Thanks, I'll have a—'

'Sauv blanc?'

She grinned. 'Please.'

He returned a few minutes later with a chilled, long-stemmed glass. 'One sauv blanc, from Western Australia I believe.' He had to raise his voice to be heard over the din. The room brimmed with laughter and good-natured bragging and jostling.

Smiling her thanks, Maggie gazed thoughtfully at the pale green-gold liquid in her glass.

Western Australia ... where Troy wants us to move to next.

She swirled the wine, pondering the aggressive recruitment strategies of the big mining companies in WA. They offered good money to lure applicants, and Troy wouldn't need much enticement to leave the Curry, she knew that for a fact.

'I'm off to the ladies.' As Lisa made her way to the amenities, a spoon tapped sharply against an empty beer glass, followed by a hiss of SHHH. The babble died down as regional director Harry and commercial works manager Jim stepped in front of the crowd.

'Right,' Harry boomed. 'Time to announce the winner of the trophy.' He turned to shake Jim's hand. 'Thanks for a good battle, Jim, but as we all know, there can only be one winner. And today,' and he raised the hastily re-touched trophy with a proud flourish, 'Corporate has emerged victorious!'

At those words a boisterous cheer arose, drowning out the few disappointed groans from the Commercial guys. The room became a moving stage of group hugs and congratulatory kisses, accompanied by tuneless renditions of 'Corporate are the Champions'.

As Tom grabbed Maggie and planted a kiss on her cheek, Grayson felt a tap on his shoulder. He turned with a smile and found Peta standing in front of him with two other women, all grinning impishly. Before he could react, Peta stood on tiptoes and kissed him on the mouth, a quick, guilty kiss that tasted of stale spirits. When she stumbled off her toes, she stood swaying and gazing boldly into his eyes until her friends dragged her away, giggling like school girls.

He turned to find Tom and Maggie laughing at him. Narrowing his eyes he growled, 'Oh I see. So that's the way it is?' and gave a roguish grin.

With a final teasing chuckle Maggie turned away, only to be grabbed around the waist by a pair of strong hands. She gave a squeak of surprise as Grayson spun her toward him and then lifted her into the air as though she weighed nothing. Grinning broadly, he eased her down again and kept his hands at her waist until she was steady on her feet. Then he cupped her chin, bent his head, and....

Oh! was all her bedazzled brain could register as he pressed his firm, warm mouth against hers. A pulsing heat flashed through her body like an electric current and her eyes closed of their own volition.

Oh yes ... YES!

When Grayson felt her melt against him, instinct took over. Moving a hand to cradle the back of her head, he deepened his kiss. The swirling volcano inside her erupted into a molten mass as with his other arm he drew her closer against his body. Her knees lost their inner cohesion and threatened to buckle beneath her. Only his hold kept her from sliding to the floor like melting jelly.

In what seemed like an out-of-body experience, she felt herself returning the pressure on her lips with increasing passion. Her hands had been resting lightly on his arms but now reached up to wrap themselves around his neck, as she willed him to—

Her shocked eyes snapped open as the rational part of her mind finally managed to shove its way through the hot fog of desire.

The instant she jerked her head back and pushed against him, he released his hold.

Her hands flew to her mouth as she backed away, breathing heavily, shocked eyes locked on his.

What the HELL just happened?

She only stopped moving when she bumped against the backs of the people behind, who were too busy celebrating to notice.

Grayson stood rigid the whole time, staring at her with a dazed expression. In his eyes she saw a reflection of her own astonishment at the ... encounter. She took a hasty glance around and was relieved to find no curious eyes looking their way.

Apart from Tom's.

After first staring at them open-mouthed, he grabbed them by an arm each, hissing, 'What do you two think you're doing?'

As though shaken out of his sensory daze by Tom's grip on his arm, Grayson turned abruptly without a word, dislodging Tom's restraining hand. Maggie remained where she stood without moving, as if numb.

'Well?' Tom's angry voice seemed to get through to her.

She lowered her eyes and dragged a quivering hand over her flushed forehead, not trusting herself to speak. And what could she say, anyway?

'Well,' Tom said again, 'I can tell you what it *looked* like—'

'Nothing!' Grayson snapped, turning back to glower at his friend. He bent his head, drew a deep breath, and then raised it again to say more calmly, 'It was nothing, old chum. Just doing what everyone else was, congratulating a team mate.' He fixed Tom with a compelling gaze as though willing him to drop the subject.

As a frowning Tom opened his mouth to respond, some of their team mates crowded in to congratulate them and he had to let go of Maggie's arm. The awkward moment passed ... although in the midst of the bear hugs and cheers, Maggie and Grayson kept finding each other's eyes. Eyes brimming with undercurrents and questions.

For Maggie, only one thing was certain. The kiss changed everything about their relationship.

And nothing.

I'm still a married woman.

What was I thinking, kissing another man like *that?*

She could see heat still smouldering in Grayson's eyes as he stood still and silent in the midst of the crowd, watching her. Her heart hammered in her chest as, moving slowly, she backed further away, mumbling to no one in particular, 'Gotta go, seeya.' Once out of the tight knot of people she whirled around and fled, only barely resisting the temptation to flat-out run.

The fresh outside air felt good. She sucked it into her lungs as she hurried home, her mind reeling and her emotions in turmoil. Even when she closed the door firmly behind her, it didn't shut out the sensation she was still bound to Grayson somehow. She closed her eyes and rested her feverish forehead on the cool surface of the door, as a voice behind her said, 'You're home early?'

She gave a start. 'Oh! Um ... yeah. I ... felt ... a bit weary so ... decided to come home.' Her guilt was like a tangible thing, a dark stain dripping from her every syllable. She swallowed, certain Troy would notice something was wrong, but all he did was give a vague nod and return his eyes to the TV.

Relief flooded through her. For once, Troy's indifference was working in her favour. The guilt was still there, though, bubbling caustically just beneath the surface and making her queasy. 'I'm going for a shower ... think I'll have an early night.'

'Okay.' He didn't look up as she hurried past and down the hallway.

Once inside the bathroom Maggie collapsed against the door, the stew of emotions still boiling inside her and hot tears making shiny tracks down her flushed face.

Were they tears of shame or some other, sinful emotion ... like lust?

She touched a trembling finger to her mouth, recalling her shameful response to Grayson's kiss. Had she *ever* responded to her husband's like that?

No, because he'd never kissed her like that.

Thinking back, she could only remember a sensation of damp, limp lips against her own, nothing like the warm firmness of Grayson's mouth. Thinking about it sent her inner volcano boiling and heaving again. She swiped the back of a hand across her tear-streaked face.

What's happening to me?

Squeezing her eyes shut, she bumped her head against the door as though trying to knock sense into it.

I didn't ask for this – whatever *this* is – to happen, and I don't want it.

She opened her eyes again to stare hard at her reflection in the bathroom mirror.

Are you sure about that?

She covered her face with her hands.

It's true, I'm unhappy and I wish ... I wish....

She took a sobbing breath.

I wish I'd waited for the man who could make me feel ... like this.

Allowing herself to re-live the sensation of Grayson's mouth against hers, the warmth of his hands, the firmness of his manly body, brought on another wave of pure pleasure. She relished the momentary euphoria until guilt rose once more to settle like a sour glob of bile in her throat.

What would Mum and Dad think if they saw me now?

She tried to swallow the guilt as her inner voice cajoled, 'More than anything else they wished for me to be happy, which I'm not. So...?'

The idea of giving in to her desires sent another heatwave shooting through her.

No. No. NO! It's wrong to even *think* about it!

Still her wayward heart pleaded, and she realised that a fire had been lit inside her.

One that would not easily be extinguished.

8

Grayson lay in bed, arms behind his head, staring at the ceiling. It was still dark, only four am, but he'd had all the sleep he was going to get. Reefing the pillow from beneath his head he punched it, splitting one of the side seams.

He was *still* having those same dreams, mostly re-runs of the row with Tina at Heathrow Airport, except now the setting would sometimes be the lawn bowls club. And sometimes it was Maggie, not Tina, backing away from him to be swallowed up by the crowd. In other dreams he stood in the midst of a staring crowd with Maggie in his arms, kissing her, uncaring they were being watched.

Maggie, whose lips held a subtle sweetness like clover honey.

Maggie, who'd melted against him until they felt like a single entity.

Maggie, whose passion had flowed into him like an electric charge, igniting his fuse into a sustained burn.

Maggie, who was married to another man.

He punched the ill-fated pillow again and swore. The way Maggie had pushed herself away from him when the kiss he'd intended to be a congratulatory peck flared into an intimate, revealing encounter, had sparked the return of those painful memories of Heathrow.

Just when he thought he might've put them behind him.

Flinging back the sheets he got up, hoping to leave the memories behind, but they followed him into the kitchen, where he turned on the kettle. And while he stood waiting for the water to boil, the memories pressed the replay button in his mind and he was once more back in Heathrow....

The airport was bustling, crowded and noisy, as usual. Busy forging a path through the throngs of arriving and departing passengers and the milling 'greeters' and 'droppers', he stopped abruptly and felt Tina bump against his back. Whirling around, he fixed her with a bewildered frown while the crowd continued surging around them, oblivious to the little island of two in their midst. 'Did I hear you right? Did you say you're *not coming?*'

'Yes,' she said breathlessly, 'that's what I've been trying to tell you, but you keep charging ahead—' She paused to gather herself and fixed him with a determined look.

'But...?' and he indicated the suitcase in her hand.

'This,' and she dragged the case forward, 'only has more

of *your* stuff in it. All *my* things are at Mum's.' At his baffled expression, she gave an exasperated sigh. 'Alright, I'll spell it out for you. I'm ... NOT ... coming ... to ... Australia.' Swallowing, she went on in a rush. 'I'm staying here, in the UK. I've m-met someone else.'

'You've *what?*' He dropped his case with a thud and stared at her. When she crossed her arms and stared mutely back at him, he hissed, 'You're telling me this *now*, Lisa, *here?* That you've *met someone else?*' His eyes hardened. 'Is this some kind of cruel joke, because if it is—'

She shook her head. 'It's no joke, Grayson.'

At her words he reeled back and threw both hands in the air, before remembering where they were. Dropping his arms to his sides he stepped close again and lowered his voice. 'When did this happen?'

Tina swallowed. This wasn't going well. She should have told her husband before this, as Nolan had suggested, but she hadn't found the right moment.

If there *was* a right moment for news of this kind.

She exhaled. 'Look, you were always at work and I was lonely. I saw so little of you, I couldn't tell if you still cared about me or not. Nolan was there, and ... and he loves me, and—'

'*Love?*' He spat the word and grabbed her by the arms. 'Don't try to sugar-coat this. If you're saying what I think you're saying, we're talking about *infidelity* and *betrayal,* Tina, pure and simple.' Straightening, he stared grimly down at her for a few tense moments and then his broad shoulders slumped. 'Guess I was hoping you'd deny it.' He took a breath and said dully, 'How long has this sordid affair been going on behind my back?'

She gazed at him with a mutinous set to her mouth until he gave her a small shake. Yelping, 'About six months!' she bunched her hands into fists, pressed them against his chest and pushed as hard as she could.

He let her go and stood shaking his head in disbelief. 'Six months....' Dragging an unsteady hand over his eyes he sucked in a breath, while the airport crowd kept flowing around them, inexorably, like a river to the sea. When he looked her way again, he saw Tina rubbing the places on her arms where his fingers had left pink marks.

Guilt kicked him in the guts. He'd never been anything but tender with his 'English rose' wife ... until now, until her admission she'd been cheating on him for months, hurting him in a way that would last a whole lot longer than a few superficial bruises.

That was still no excuse to get physical with her.

'I'm sorry,' he ground out, 'I didn't mean to hurt you. It's just...,' and he shook his head again, '*six* months....'

A belligerent look flashed across her pretty face. 'Well, if you'd spent more time at home you might've realised earlier what was happening, like your friends did—'

'WHAT?'

She jumped, startled by the harsh intensity of that one staccato word, and then resentment rose within her. Meeting his reproachful stare, she muttered sullenly, 'That's right, your so-called friends knew about me and Nolan. Some even invited us out as a couple.'

'I don't believe it.' His eyes narrowed. 'Someone would have said something—'

She gave a humourless laugh. 'Yes, they might've, if you'd given them a chance. As it was, they were like me, never knowing when you'd next have time for them.'

'*Time?*' His voice rose. 'What time did I have for *anyone*, Tina, myself included?'

She cringed and waved at him to lower his voice.

When he spoke again his voice was low and hard. 'You weren't working, and I was expected to keep you in the *manner* to which you were accustomed, something your parents made very clear to me before you and I married.' He pressed his lips into a hard line. 'That kind of lifestyle costs money, money we only had if I worked every contract and every bit of overtime I was offered. And in my line of work, that means travelling to construction sites and being away from home a lot of the time. Not by *choice*, by the way.' Raking a hand through his hair, he added, 'Of course someone from a silver-spoon background like yours can't comprehend having to work for every shilling.'

When she didn't speak, he gave a grim snort. 'More fool me, living a life forced on me by others. Exactly what I thought I'd left behind when I moved out of home.' He shook his head again and fixed her with incredulous eyes. 'I did it thinking I could keep everyone happy, and look what it got me. A cheating wife who says it's all my fault for working too much, and a bunch of friends happy to go along with her betrayal. *Unbelievable.*'

'Grayson—'

'Enough!' He raised a hand. 'I've heard enough.' As he struggled to get his feelings under control, he discovered a puzzling sense of inevitability beneath the shock and hurt. Had he somehow known, subconsciously, that this would happen? That the prettiest girl in his class at school, the one he'd had a crush on for what felt like forever and pursued until they became a couple, would end up casting him off for another man?

Without looking at her he said in a flat, resigned tone, 'There's no hope for us anymore? You and I are finished?'

Seeing her slow nod, he hung his head. A moment later the first call for the flight to Sydney came over the airport's PA system.

'So ... what are you going to do?' Her voice was choked with emotion.

Lifting his head, he eyed her sadly, thinking how far they'd come in such a short time. Was it really just hours ago they'd handed back the keys to 'Cherry Cottage', their home for three years, before heading to the airport and their 'bright new future'? Come to think of it, Tina *had* been quiet and withdrawn on the drive there. *He* was the excited one.

'That's our ... *my* ... plane,' he said gruffly, 'I have to go.'

When he bent to collect his suitcase she put a soft hand on his arm. 'You're still going to Australia?' Feeling him stiffen she let her hand slip to her side.

'May as well,' he growled, 'what have I got to hold me here now?' He turned on his heel, about to hurry to the check-in counter, and then paused. Sighing, he half-turned to say over a shoulder, 'Will you be alright? Are you going to stay at your mother's?'

'Initially.' Her breath caught in her throat. 'Then ... Nolan and I are moving in together—'

His face darkened. 'Right then.'

In the gruff words she heard reproach and a touching bewilderment, and as she watched him stride away to become swallowed up by the crowd, a single tear traced a wet path down her expensively preserved English rose complexion.

'So mate, d'you wanna talk about it?' Tom eyed Grayson. It looked like he'd spent a rough night.

'No.'

Tom gave a small shrug. 'Well, when or if you do, you know where to find me.'

'I don't need to hear your accusations or anyone else's.' Grayson's frown deepened. 'I'm laying them on thickly enough for myself.'

Turning, Tom closed the office door and then took a seat in front of the desk. 'Am I right in thinkin' we're talkin' about what happened between you and Maggie?' At Grayson's curt nod he leaned back, both hands behind his head. 'Look, Reevers, let's put this into perspective. We're only talkin' about a kiss, right? Just one kiss?'

Grayson shot him a narrow-eyed glance but didn't speak.

'At a time when everybody was kissing somebody.' Tom

shrugged. 'Yours was more than a quick peck, it's true, but in the heat of the moment—'

Grayson gave an annoyed grunt and shook his head. 'You don't understand.'

'What don't I understand? That you're attracted to her? I'm not blind, man!'

'Attracted?' Grayson raised his eyes to the ceiling. 'I guess you could call it that.'

'Okay, so you and Maggie are attracted to each other—'

'Hang on, you can't assume to know how Maggie feels.'

'Well,' Tom said drily, 'it sure looked like mutual attraction to me.'

A look akin to hope crossed Grayson's face. He quickly squashed it. 'That doesn't matter. What does matter is that it shouldn't have happened. Neither of us is free to ... do things like that.'

'What do you mean, *neither* of you? Aren't you and Tina divorced?'

'Yes, but that doesn't mean I've forgotten what she did.' A bitter note crept into Grayson's voice. 'And I haven't been able to trust another woman since ... not in *that* way, anyhow.'

'Ah, yes, well....' Tom paused. 'Maybe your situation is easier than you think.'

'*Easier?* What do you mean by that?' Grayson flicked him an accusing glance. 'I hope you're not suggesting an affair?' His expression darkened. 'I know how lousy it feels to be on the wrong end of one, so I'd never even *consider* doing that to another chap.' He scowled and bit his lip, angry with himself for divulging so much.

Tom fixed him with a level gaze. 'I'm not condoning any funny business, I don't want to see either of you hurt. What I mean is, Maggie's married. You can't have her, it's that simple. But you *can* admire her from afar, like others have.'

Grayson gave a humourless laugh. 'You make it sound so logical.'

'I hear a "but" coming?'

'But ... while that's *exactly* what I should be doing – admiring her from afar and nothing more – I don't think I can.'

'Why not?'

'Because....' Grayson exhaled and sat forward. Resting his forearms on the desk, he stared down at its laminate surface without seeing it. Shaking his head slowly, he mumbled, 'That's not enough any more.'

Sunday, 11:17:49 AM

From: Maggie.Perkins@home

To: Eviebird@myplace

Subject: Re: Help!

Can I chew your ear again, Evie? I need to talk this through some more and you're the only person I can trust to keep it *absolutely* confidential. We both know you don't care much for Troy, but I don't want him hearing about this 'incident' and being hurt by my stupidity. And before you tell me again you think it was romantic, not foolish, just remember – I'm a married woman and yet I kissed another man. And I mean

REALLY kissed him. I still can't believe I did that ... it all feels kind of surreal.

And wrong.

So, what now? I can hardly look Troy in the face, knowing what I've done. And it's not only the kiss, it's how I *felt* about the kiss. It was like I'd been waiting for it my whole life. And you know what? Even the simple act of admitting that to you has the guilt seeping into my atoms like arsenic.

I'm sorry if I'm rambling, but I have so many questions and so few answers.

I don't know myself anymore ... and I don't know Grayson either. He was affected by the kiss, there's no denying that, but it could've been a simple case of lust – for him at least. There's more going on with me that I don't quite understand. Anyway, there's no way I would overturn my life on a whim and cause a lot of hurt in the process. Troy certainly doesn't deserve that. Oh sure, he's the wrong man for me, but I'm to blame for our being together. After all, nobody *made* me marry him. In fact, I clearly remember you *ordering* me not to! And I love you for that, and so much more.

I have to keep trying to make this marriage work, Evie, there's nothing else for it. I know you think I'm wasting my time, but Troy is my husband, I made a lifelong commitment to him.

So ... in an attempt to ease my guilty conscience, I'm making him a special dinner tonight and going the whole hog – candles, wine, soft music. I'll let you know how it went.

Maggie x

=====================

. . .

Sunday, 10:35:06 PM

From: Maggie.Perkins@home

To: Eviebird@myplace

Subject: Re: Re: Help!

Well, I spent the whole afternoon preparing our special dinner but I guess it made more of an impression on me than it did on Troy. He got home late and made no comment when he saw my carefully spread table (I used my favourite white tablecloth and polished the glassware 'til it gleamed).

He didn't do justice to the meal either. He picked at it, saying he wasn't all that hungry, and then got up from the table to flop on the lounge in front of the TV. Five minutes later he asked me to get him a packet of potato chips from the pantry! So it wasn't that he had no appetite, he just didn't want what I was offering.

All the trouble I'd gone to was for nothing. I could've cried, Evie, only I was too angry.

And so arises the ultimate question, which sums up all my recent ramblings and is never far from my mind – I can feel it there, dug in like the spore of a noxious weed – can Troy and I make this marriage work, or is it already beyond saving?

Maggie x

====================

'What can I getcha, Mags?' The shopkeeper beamed a welcome as she came through the door and went to the chiller section.

'Just some milk, thanks Dave.'

'Put that bottle back, love. We just got a delivery of some fresh stuff, I'll grab ya'one of those.' He disappeared into the back room and re-emerged holding a chill-frosted white bottle. 'There ya'go.' Holding it out, he gave her a wink. 'Use-by date *ages* away.'

She smiled, wondering if he'd ever stop treating her like royalty. It seemed he'd never forget how she'd helped place his daughter into an administrative traineeship with the department. Like most Cloncurry parents, he was dreading having his precious offspring leave home to find work, followed by the inevitable long distance phone calls and days spent travelling to check on her.

'Thanks.' She handed over the money and headed back to the office.

Later, after managing to avoid discussing the lawn bowls competition and its after-party with her colleagues, she was dismayed to see engineer Bob Evans making a bee-line for her office.

Close to retirement age, crusty, small town bachelor Bob had settled comfortably into the role of resident gossip. If there were something a person didn't want seen, Bob would be the one to see it ... and tell the world about it.

Coming in to stand uncomfortably close to Maggie, he said, 'That was some bowls comp, hey?'

She rolled her office chair away until it hit the desk

behind. Undeterred, he moved in close again to snigger, 'And how about the after party? What a turn-up that proved to be!'

Her heart sank.

What did he see? What does he know?

Swallowing, she said, 'Yes, quite a night.'

'And even more so for some—'

'What do you mean by that?'

He winked. 'I would've thought *you'd* know, Maggie?'

Oh no....

'Look, Bob—'

'What a scandal!'

She blanched.

'And her a married woman and all.'

Her! He said *her*, not *you*.

She took a calming breath. 'Bob, I'm not interested in gossip, you know that.'

'Oh, but this might have workplace ramifications. That's why I thought you would've known about it, being our HR person 'n all.'

Sweet relief trickled into her veins but she had to make sure it wasn't premature. 'Alright Bob, get to the point. What's this all about?'

When he leaned in close again, she had to resist the urge to twist away. His breath reeked of cigarette smoke, tooth decay and stale garlic, and she fought to keep the revulsion from showing on her face.

'Well, as it turns out, Peta has a case of the hots for the new guy, Grayson.'

'Old news, Bob.'

'Ah, but that's only the start. It appears she might have had a knock-back from the gentleman in question.' He frowned and licked his lips. The saliva clung there in a glistening line. 'Although my sources didn't actually witness this, they did see what happened next.' His body language was all delight.

She couldn't help screwing up her face in disgust.

Bob didn't notice, so blissfully engrossed was he in someone else's business. 'So, she took her – wares? – to the next highest bidder. And it wasn't Roger, her other half, oh no! It was—'

'Enough, Bob! All I need to know is whether this other party was a staff member.'

'Well, no, but—'

'Right then.' She lifted her chin. 'This has nothing to do with me or the department.'

'But—'

'But nothing, Bob. What you're talking about is a private matter, and that's the end of it.'

'So you don't want to know who she—'

'No, I don't want to know. And Bob, it's none of your business or anyone else's for that matter.' Swallowing a grin at his obvious disappointment, she gave a curt nod and turned her back, signalling an end to the discussion.

After he'd marched out of her office with an irritated huff, she slumped in her chair.

That was close.

She bent her head to rub her eyes and pinch the bridge of her nose.

Look at what I've become, a paranoid cheater. Well, maybe cheater is too strong a word. It *was* just a kiss, a once-off, heat of the moment thing. But I still feel like I've cheated on Troy.

She let her hand drop and raised her head.

I need to stop being so melodramatic, and just keep my distance from Grayson. That shouldn't be hard, it's already days since he's been anywhere near me.

Wait! What if he's avoiding me, perhaps even blames me for what happened?

Her stomach clenched and she once more saw herself melting against him, giving herself up to his kiss. Wincing as though in pain, she squeezed her eyes tightly shut and covered her face with her hands.

Oh no, what does he think of me? A married woman, kissing him like that. Crap, crap, cr—

'Maggie?'

She jumped and spun around, to see the regional director standing in her office doorway looking concerned.

'Oh! Hi Harry.'

'Is everything okay?'

'Oh, yeah ... everything's fine. I'm just a bit tired, that's all.'

He walked over to her desk, gazing down at her with a fatherly expression. 'It's been a busy time for you. I hope you're looking after yourself.'

'Yes, *Dad*.' She grinned up at him.

'Okay, enough of that.' He gave a quick smile and leaned

against the edge of her desk, crossing his arms and ankles. 'I've come to talk to you about Megan's promotion.'

Relieved to be back on a professional footing, Maggie said evenly, 'Harry, I don't think promoting her so soon is a good idea, especially as there are other, longer serving officers more deserving of promotion whose noses you'd be putting out of joint. Megan's been pushing for a promotion since day one, and while she's a clever and capable administration officer, I've also witnessed her displaying some unprofessional behaviour.'

'Shouldn't we reward her good performance? Her current supervisor's happy with how she's been going so far.'

When Harry pulled up a chair and sat in it, Maggie smiled inwardly. It made a nice change having the RD sit down with her. His busy schedule usually didn't allow for much more than quick catch-ups, often during chance meetings in the staff room between appointments.

After a lengthy discussion on the benefits and drawbacks of promoting junior staff, Harry rose to his feet with a nod. 'Thanks for your advice, Maggie. I think you're right. We'll put a hold on Megan's promotion for now, and see how she goes tempering her raw ambition with professionalism and self-control. Now I'd better get back to my office before Samantha comes looking for me.' He threw her a wink. 'A dog with a bone, that secretary of mine.' He headed to the doorway and paused to look back. 'Oh yeah, I also meant to find out when you're taking that trip to the gulf?'

Her stomach turned over. A trip like that would mean

travelling in close confines with Grayson, precisely what she – and possibly Grayson as well – was trying to avoid.

Harry saw her screw up her face. 'What's wrong? I thought you said you'd be happy to go and take Grayson for a look-see?' When she stared at him without speaking, he frowned. 'I've already made the commitment, Maggie. I need someone with your expertise up there, and I don't have time to find a replacement at such short notice.'

'Sorry, Harry. It just ... slipped my mind.' She took a ragged breath. 'Will next week be soon enough?'

'Fine. As we discussed before, I want you to ascertain the situation up there. Some of the reports I've received about the behaviour of the road crews are quite concerning.'

Maggie was barely listening. She'd heard it all before anyway and her mind was otherwise occupied, picturing herself and Grayson together, at close quarters, for the better part of a week. And alone for a lot of the time.

That's just great.

She sighed.

So much for keeping our distance....

At the tentative knock on his office door, Grayson looked up from where he and two other engineers were bent over the drawing spread across his desk. On seeing Maggie in the doorway, he straightened and gave a stiff nod in greeting.

The other two men shifted in their seats, sensing a growing tension in the room. With a quick glance at Grayson, they rose and retreated with a mumbled, 'Hi Maggie,' as they passed.

She threw them a tight smile and stepped into the office to stand in front of the desk, hands clasped in front of her at first and then hidden behind her back, in case they weren't quite steady. She'd had to rally her courage to approach Grayson, having not spoken to him since the infamous lawn bowls incident. And she would still be keeping away if not for Harry's ultimatum about their gulf trip.

'Hi Grayson.'

'Maggie.' He sat back to fix her with a hooded, contemplative gaze.

She swallowed. 'I need to talk to you about the gulf trip I mentioned before, you remember?'

'I remember.'

'Okay. Well, Harry wants it to happen soon, as in next week.'

'I see.'

'So can we talk over the arrangements, if you've got time?'

He indicated the chair facing his desk and she perched herself on the edge, her body taut as though poised to flee. Their conversation was brief and business-like, their words stilted, eye contact avoided wherever possible.

Relieved when all the details had been thrashed out, she nodded and rose to go. In her haste to escape the tension hanging heavy in the room, she turned too quickly and caught her foot in the leg of the chair. Lurching sideways, she came dangerously close to falling nose-first into the boot-scuffed carpet, but managed to fling out her arms and career into the wall.

Grayson had leapt to his feet the moment she tripped, but stopped dead when she thrust out a halting hand.

Face ablaze, she straightened, threw him an agonised look, and rushed out without another word. As she dashed to her office, mortified, ears peeled for the humiliating guffaws of laughter she was sure would erupt behind her, all she heard were the usual office sounds of busy keyboards and energetic paper-pushing. And if she'd looked back, she would have seen Grayson standing in his doorway watching her hurry away.

Not laughing.

Not even smiling.

But she hadn't looked back, nor to left or right. She kept her eyes downcast and her mind fixed on reaching the safety of her desk. Once there, she collapsed into the chair and put her head in her hands, willing herself to forget the face-flaming, stomach-turning episode.

At least we managed to agree on a date for the dreaded trip, she told herself, so my ridiculous 'performance' wasn't in vain.

Sure, but on the long, long road to the gulf there'll be no escaping the awkwardness between us.

9

The driver of the dusty ute raised a hand as the two vehicles passed on the Burke Developmental Road. Grayson returned the greeting without comment, having grown familiar with the fellowship of strangers in the outback, the fleeting connection between travellers, the reminder they were still part of the human race while traversing the 'back of beyond'.

As they headed north toward Burketown in the gulf, Maggie stared at the passing scenery, trying to focus her attention away from the man in the driver's seat. His strong, capable hands on the steering wheel skilfully guided the fast-moving 4WD along the highway. The vehicle's high-clearance suspension made it bounce as they crossed Capsize Creek near Quamby.

She was glad Grayson had arranged a wagon instead of

one of the dual cab utes, which were more workmanlike but less comfortable on long trips. He'd scored another point too, by asking if she wanted to drive. While happy enough for him to 'captain' the trip, she was pleased he hadn't simply assumed he would because he was the man.

And now they'd left Cloncurry behind and were on the open highway. She risked a quick glance at him from under her lashes. How could he look so damn composed when she was feeling anything but?

She turned away again.

I shouldn't be irritated by his composure, I should be glad he isn't allowing the awkwardness between us to affect his driving.

The car's nose dipped suddenly as Grayson took his foot off the accelerator. 'Hey, look at that!' He pointed to a flock of tiny birds settling like a bright green mist into clumps of long grass on the roadside.

She leaned forward to see them better and breathed, 'Oh, how beautiful.'

Grayson slowed the car further. 'I wonder what kind of birds they are?'

'Finches, I think.'

'What sort?'

'Green ones.' She smiled, her gaze still on the drooping blades of bird-filled grass. 'Kidding. I like birds, but I don't know particular breeds, apart from common ones like the Indian Mina and the house sparrow. Of course they're not pretty like these little guys.'

He grinned and they shared a moment of mutual enjoyment before an undercurrent passed between them. Their smiles dissolved and they turned away in unison, as if on cue.

She groaned inwardly.

This is like an act in a bad play, and we're only at Act One. It's going to be one heck of a long performance.

Sighing, she gazed out the window at the passing stands of blue gums, salt bush, majestic ghost gums shedding their bark like torn cream lace, and patches of mallee scrub. When they crossed the bridge over Dismal Creek, Grayson's deep voice broke into her reverie.

'We'll stop at Burke and Wills Roadhouse, yeah?' At her silent nod he added hastily, 'But if you need to stop sooner—'

'No!' She gave herself a mental kick and cleared her throat. Snapping at him went against her commitment to keep her cool. Besides, he was only being considerate, even if the state of her bladder was none of his business. 'The roadhouse will be fine, thanks.'

And that's when she felt the first hint of a need.

Damn, Grayson. Now look what you've started.

It wasn't fair to blame him, the fault lay with the power of suggestion. Either way she was determined not to request a special stop, not even for a fretful bladder. She refused to add weight to the general consensus that women need more comfort stops on a journey. What difference did gender make in that equation anyway?

There was another consideration too, the lack of amenities along that stretch of road. It didn't even offer many shrubs bushy enough to provide sufficient screening. That left her with one option – to not make the situation worse. Limiting her fluid intake might go against what was taught in the department's 'Working in Hot Environments' sessions, but it would enable her to make it to the roadhouse without a stop.

'So, is the roadhouse named after the famous explorers, Burke and Wills?' His eyes were on the road but he sounded genuinely interested.

'Yes, but it's also called that 'cos it's at the junction of the Burke Developmental and Wills Developmental Roads, what the locals call the "Four Ways".'

At his nod, she looked out the window again. 'I like the thought of naming places as a tribute to the early explorers. Especially as some, like Burke and Wills, perished without realising how close they'd come to reaching their goals.'

'And the "Four Ways" is where we turn to head to Gregory?'

'Yep. After that the road is mostly gravel all the way to Burketown.'

Silence returned to the car's cabin.

Passing through Three Rivers, Grayson slowed when he noticed names painted in large white letters on a mound of boulders by the side of the road. He gave an amused grunt. 'Obviously "Stumpy", "Wookie" and "Muck" were on the construction or maintenance crew for this section of roadway.' He eyed the graffiti as they passed. 'And that looks remarkably like departmental line-marking paint.'

It didn't sound like he expected an answer so Maggie remained silent as they accelerated to highway speed again. Her mouth and throat were dry, and she could feel the beginnings of a dehydration headache. She resisted the urge to moisten her lips with her tongue, which merely rasped over their parched surface.

It may have been a bad idea to stop drinking....

Grayson must have noticed she was abstaining for at one stage he offered her a drink from his own water bottle. She thanked him but refused, knowing the roadhouse wasn't far away.

As soon as they arrived she headed for the amenities. Coming out, she saw him at the café counter paying for a bottle of chilled water. When she walked over to join him, he handed her the bottle with a reproving glance as if to say *and I expect you to drink it.*

Feeling a rise of irritation at his officiousness, she merely nodded her thanks as he turned back to the woman behind the counter. When he ordered coffees and home-made melting-moment biscuits, her irritation melted away.

Coffee and a melting-moment ... a man after my own heart.

Damn!

Since when am I a parrot, easily won over by a biscuit?

Glancing at the glass biscuit barrel on the counter and seeing glossy white cream oozing temptingly from between golden shortbread rounds, she smacked her lips.

Polly wanna melting moment?

'Would you like to eat inside, or out on the veranda?'

The smile in his deep voice, combined with the aromatic steam rising from the coffees in his hands and the prospect of a favourite sweet biscuit to enjoy, made her feel ... better.

Maybe this won't be so bad after all. I should just follow his lead and make the best of the situation.

'Outside, if it's not too hot for you.' She looked up at him with raised brows and a tentative smile.

He shrugged. 'Okay by me.'

They made their way to a battered wooden table at the end of the veranda and sat on opposite sides. Squawking Apostle birds immediately mobbed them, hopping around the table looking for handouts. Maggie threw crumbs their way while sipping her coffee.

Another noisy group of the birds had congregated around a puddle beneath a nearby rain water tank. Grayson pointed to them. 'Any port in a storm, eh?'

She nodded. 'Water is a precious commodity out here.' Spying movement in the long grass behind the tank, she peered closer and then pointed. 'Hey, look! A rock wallaby. There, in the paddock.'

Grayson got up and went to the edge of the veranda to get a look at his first Australian rock wallaby. As he rested a foot on the bottom rung and leaned his arms on the railing, Maggie popped the last delicious morsel of biscuit into her mouth and stared at his broad back.

Well, if I had to be tempted by another man, at least I chose a worthy specimen.

She frowned and hung her head. Grayson was putting in an effort to remain professional and civil. She *had* to follow suit ... or die trying, her melodramatic side added for good measure.

Grayson turned and tossed some biscuit crumbs to a brash Apostle bird that had ventured close to his work-booted feet. His eyes fell on the colourful posters the road-house owners had pinned to the outside wall – hoping to stave off repetitious questions about the area's wildlife from curious tourists no doubt – and he moved closer to read them.

Maggie left him engrossed and headed to the ladies for a final freshen-up. She splashed her face with water and let the droplets evaporate, savouring the brief coolness on her heat-flushed skin. Staring into the stained mirror, she narrowed her eyes at her reflection.

You *will* regard Grayson as just another work colleague, and treat him accordingly.

With a resolute nod, she dried her hands on a paper towel and strode out to find him once more at the counter of the café, this time ordering lunch to take away.

When she reached his side he looked down at her. 'What will you have?'

The warm light in his grey eyes made her throat tighten. The seconds ticked by before she finally stuttered, 'Wh-whatever you're having ... will be fine by me as well.'

When he nodded and turned to address the woman behind the counter again, Maggie cringed inwardly, hoping she hadn't committed to eating the roadhouse's infamously fiery chilli beef, or a three-day-old gristly meat pie of uncertain origin. Then she saw the woman split two crusty bread rolls and begin filling them with slivers of roast beef, crisp lettuce, thick slices of ripe tomato, red-gold shredded carrot, and chunky relish, and breathed a sigh of relief.

Tasty and much healthier than Troy's standard road trip tucker of greasy chips and fried kabana.

The sweating woman placed the rolls, now filled to bursting, into a large paper bag along with two orange-and-poppy-seed muffins and some fresh fruit. After pouring boiling water into Grayson's thermos, she loaded it, paper cups, tea bags, milk sachets and the bag of food, into a cardboard box. Then, brushing a lock of straggly hair off her damp face with the back of a buttery hand, she bestowed a coy, gap-toothed smile on Grayson. 'You buggars are lucky we just got our fresh order in.' She handed him his change. 'If the road'd been closed again, I'd have been offering youse microwaved pies or a fry-up at best.'

Thanking her and taking the box of provisions from the counter, Grayson led the way back to the car. Its interior was stifling despite the shady park. After placing the box on the back seat, he promptly started the engine so the air conditioner could begin cooling the cabin.

As Maggie settled into the passenger's seat, she sensed a dampening of their awkwardness with each other. The coffee-n-biscuit cure, perhaps?

Sobering, she glanced sideways at Grayson.

He's simply a work colleague – I mustn't lose sight of that.

· · ·

Not long after taking the turn onto the Wills Developmental Road they hit a straight stretch, and up ahead Grayson saw an emergency airstrip painted on the bitumen. When he raised his eyebrows at her, Maggie said, 'For the Flying Doctors and other emergency landings.'

He nodded his approval. 'A jolly good idea. I can't imagine there'd be many airports or other options for safe landings out here.'

Slowing as they rolled into the tiny township of Gregory Downs a short time later, he nosed the car onto the verge near where a crew was working on a new stretch of road, and looked over at Maggie. 'Do you mind? I'd like to hear what work's being done up here.'

'Not at all.'

When he called up the supervisor on the two-way, a deep voice boomed back, 'Big George 'ere. I'm in the grader. Give me a sec 'n I'll meet yez at the site hut.'

At Grayson's low chuckle, Maggie threw him a questioning glance.

'It's nothing really, just something Tom said about Big George.'

'Oh yeah?'

'Do you know him?'

She shook her head. 'He's with the Commercial group and out on site most of the time.'

'Well, George is a site supervisor, so grading isn't part of his duties. But the chaps reckon he can't resist taking a turn in the grader whenever he can. Seems he enjoys playing with big toys.'

'Like a lot of blokes.'

Grayson gave a wry grin. 'Right.'

Climbing out of the car at the site hut a short time later, Maggie raised her arms and stretched, as a work ute pulled in beside them. When the driver emerged, she could see the reason for his nickname. Of Aboriginal descent, Big George was shorter than Grayson but considerably wider. His dusty face broke into a broad, white smile as he heaved his bulky body in its grubby work clobber in the direction of the site hut, signalling for them to follow.

'Come, have a cuppa wit' me.'

His billy tea was sweet, black, and served in chipped pannikins of somewhat dubious cleanliness. After handing out the drinks, George flopped his bulk into a battered chair, and with the box air conditioner banging away in the corner of the demountable, sipped his tea and chatted to them like old friends.

They were almost reluctant to leave. George too seemed sorry to see them go, despite his eagerness to get back to grading. But they all knew this was not a road to travel at night in a passenger vehicle.

'Unfenced,' Big George said, 'dat's why dere's so many of dem cattle grids embedded in da bitumen.'

Grayson nodded. 'We've seen some strays already. Lone beasts and even whole herds.'

'Yeah, 'n piles of bones 'n hides by da roadside. Road kill, all picked clean 'n left to dry in da sun.' George slapped Grayson on the shoulder and dipped his head at Maggie. 'You go safe now, y'hear?'

Not long after setting off again, as though to prove Big George right, they passed a fresh carcass on the side of the road. Their arrival disturbed the three enormous eagles feasting on the road kill. They took flight, feathered legs and taloned feet in full view under their vast outstretched wings. As the car passed beneath the birds, Maggie and Grayson shared an awed glance before quickly looking up again, to watch the dark bodies become specks in the sky above.

'Cripes, those falcons are a size!'

'Ah ... they're not falcons, Gray, they're wedge-tailed eagles.'

'Wedge-tails? Wow.'

Still gazing skyward Maggie sang softly, 'Look at me, I'm a wedge-tail ... don't you wish you could windsail....'

'What's that?'

She blinked and colour infused her cheeks. 'A song by John Williamson.' At his quizzical look, she said, 'Have you heard any of his music? He's recorded a heap of albums.'

Grayson shook his head.

'Then you need to. His songs are compulsory listening for all new Aussies.' She looked up at the black specks disappearing from sight. 'I read somewhere that wedge-tails can have a wingspan of over two metres.'

'You Aussies don't do anything by halves, do you?' They

shared a laugh and Grayson teased, 'I thought you didn't know anything about birds?' His eyes held a warm smile that heightened the rosy blush in her cheeks.

She hastily turned to look out the window again. 'One thing I do know is that the wildlife and the beauty we encounter out here never fails to surprise and delight me.'

He gave a slow nod, his gaze lingering on her profile.

As the kilometres sped away beneath their wheels, Maggie eyed the changing countryside. Fewer trees dotted the horizon and the flat geography gave the land a 'mud flats' feel.

'Which I always find ironic,' she said when mentioning it to Grayson, 'considering how dry and hot it is up here. But the monsoon can turn that around *real* quick.'

'Oh yes?'

'Yeah. When the "big wet" hits, the creeks and rivers often burst their banks right out of the blue, and the terrain's flatness makes the roads easy targets for flash flooding.'

'What time of year does that happen?'

'Mostly in summer, but floods are possible at other times too, especially if a late cyclone hits the coast and comes across as a rain depression. That happened a couple of years ago, cutting Cloncurry off by road in all four directions. The only way in and out of town was by plane. Luckily, the airport had been built on high ground. John Flynn's Flying Doctors needed a reliable runway.' She glanced over at him and said brightly, 'Did you know the service had its start in Cloncurry, along with QANTAS?'

He gave a dip of his head, and as he gazed into her animated face, a tender smile hovered around his mouth. Her heart turned over on seeing it.

Careful ... just another colleague, remember.

She swallowed and charged on. 'It was quite late in the season when those floods happened – around this time of year if I remember right. It was like the sting in the end of summer's tail. Something good came of it though. The water made its way to Lake Eyre and filled it for the first time in ... I don't know how many years.'

He was about to say something when a large object shimmered into view on the horizon. Seeing a pilot car emerge from the heat haze followed by a semi hauling a large, wide load, he turned up the volume on the car's two-way radio and grabbed the handpiece.

Amid the static the pilot's scratchy voice came over the radio, announcing, 'Small vehicle, heading north.'

The semi driver answered immediately. 'Right-o, I'll watch out for 'im.'

Grayson spoke into the handpiece. 'Pilot vehicle, this is Main Roads two five six on Wills Developmental Road heading for Burketown, over.'

'G'day mate. Good to hear another voice. Apart from Boofhead's, of course, in the big boy back there. Gets mighty lonely on this road, over.'

'What are you hauling? Over.'

'Mining equipment, for the new copper mine, over.'

When Maggie leaned closer to whisper, 'A newly commissioned mine north-east of Cloncurry,' her nose caught Grayson's scent and she hastily withdrew. Despite the heat, he smelled fresh but also warm and wholesome, like a coffee plantation washed with summer rain.

Giving herself a mental slap, she inched as far away from him as her seat would allow. She ended up scrunched against the car door.

Now I'm being ridiculous.

Wriggling to settle herself more comfortably, she shot him a sideways glance and was thankful his attention had remained on the road and the two-way, which crackled with the pilot's voice once more.

'You should be right to pass when you get to the big boy, this is a fairly wide bit of highway. Not like some of the stuff you're going to hit soon, over.'

'So what are we in for? Over.'

'Narrow gravel and lots of it between here and Burketown. Plenty of stray cattle too, to help you stay awake, over.'

'Thanks for the heads-up, cobber. Over.'

'You a Pom, mate? Over.'

'Right you are, over.'

'Well even Poms are welcome here,' and the pilot's voice took on a lyrical note, 'in the *better* hemisphere. How's that, Boofhead?' The heavy hauler driver could be heard chortling. 'Hah! I'm a poet and I didn't even know it! Over.'

Grayson gave a bark of laughter and winked at Maggie, before countering with an exaggerated British accent. 'Jolly good, chaps. Her Majesty sends her regards to you colonials by the way, and wonders when you're coming home to collect your pardons, over.'

This met with loud, static-filled guffaws from both drivers.

'Touché, mate!' the heavy hauler driver hollered.

Still chuckling, the pilot said, 'Hey, Brit, I hope you brought some music with ya, 'cos you're about to lose your AM/FM radio reception. Luckily you'll have UHF all the way. Over.' And right on cue, the music playing softly through the car's speakers spluttered and became a static buzz.

Grayson switched off the radio and raised an eyebrow at Maggie. Mimicking Yoda from *Star Wars,* he declared, 'Prepared for this, I was,' and pointed to the glove compartment under the car's dashboard.

Her eyes widened at his woeful attempt at mimicry and she laughed aloud.

When he grinned and prompted, 'Music,' she opened the compartment and found a selection of CDs. 'Go ahead, choose one.'

She took the album closest to the top and inserted the disc into the player. Almost immediately, a Cold Play hit song throbbed from the speakers.

As they passed the semi and its pilot in a cloud of road verge dust, Grayson wished them a safe trip over the two-way.

. . .

When they hit a recently-graded section of gravel a while later, Maggie took the opportunity to make their cups of tea. She managed not to spill any, which was quite a feat on an unsealed road prone to bone and teeth-shaking corrugation. Handing one to Grayson, she settled back to sip from her steaming mug and gaze out the window again.

As they passed the sign to Boomarra Station near Quail Creek, Grayson indicated the crack-patching on the bitumen seal. 'Would the damage have resulted from the flash flooding you were telling me about before?'

'Quite probably. All the water rushing over and under the road seal doesn't do it much good, as I'm sure you know.'

He nodded, and they didn't speak again until she spotted a sign ahead.

'Do you want to stop at the Gregory River crossing, like Big George suggested?' She smiled. 'This might be the only chance to dip those British toes of yours in some real gulf country water.'

He grinned back at her. 'Sure. Just for a minute though, time's getting away from us.'

The Gregory River, a precious oasis in the sweltering harshness of the gulf country, meandered alongside the road like a thick green snake, tempting hot, dusty travellers with its watery serenity. At one bridge, they saw three majestic brolgas standing in the shade of willows at the river's edge. The graceful trees overhung the river, dangling their leafy fingers in the clear green water.

At the crossing, a popular camping spot, Grayson drove onto the pebbly riverbank and parked in a patch of shade.

When he turned off the ignition they could hear the nearby gurgle of swirling water, and wasted no time getting out and having a stretch. The sight of the river bubbling over smooth stones, the water in places a deep bottle-green in the shade of dangling willows, was too tempting to refuse. Maggie made her way to the bank, where she kicked off her shoes and dipped a tentative toe in the water. It was delightfully cool. She rolled up her cargo pants and waded in, feeling the smooth river stones underfoot and the water washing away the dust and heat from her skin.

Calling over a shoulder, 'C'mon, Gray, the water's fine! Oh, and there aren't any crocodiles in the Gregory,' she waded further out to stand knee-deep in the swirling water. 'Oh yeah, this is great.'

'It sure is.' He waded past her into a deeper part of the river, the legs of his work pants rolled up to his knees.

They bent to splash the cool water over their arms and faces. When she glimpsed a tiny bird fly between them, mere inches above the water, she paused to watch it dart into tall reeds growing near the edge. How good it felt to be sharing these experiences with Grayson. And not just good, it felt *right*. When he glanced her way with a broad smile, she couldn't resist splashing water at him with an impish giggle.

He gave a sharp intake of breath and then grinned. 'Be careful not to start something you can't finish, young lady!' Opening his arms like a sumo wrestler, he charged at her through the water, only to stop mid-stream when he realised what he was doing, and how it must look. And in that instant it seemed to both of them that everything stilled, except the flowing river. It caught and rushed downstream those moments of innocent pleasure, taking them out of reach.

They stood with eyes locked together, while the longing, guilt and regret swirled around them like the waters of the Gregory. Maggie blinked and released the air held in her lungs in a long, shuddering breath. Grayson remained where he stood, unmoving, his eyes burning into hers with an almost unbearable intensity. Squeezing her own eyes shut, she raised her hands as though warding off danger. When she heard him wading through the water toward her, she snapped her eyes open again to find him standing a mere arm's length away.

When he extended a hand, she slowly raised sad eyes to his and shook her head ever so slightly.

And the precious interlude at the river became just another poignant memory.

She turned to splash her way to the bank and then drip a wet trail to the car. She didn't see his angry headshake behind her, nor hear him cursing under his breath for breaking his own promise.

For the rest of the trip Grayson stared fixedly at the road ahead, while Maggie gazed out her side window at the gradually dimming landscape. She was thankful for the road noise, air conditioner hiss, and Cold Play hits to soften the prickly silence.

They were both relieved to arrive in Burketown.

When they checked in at the hotel, the receptionist said, 'We have you booked into separate cabins, is that right?' She looked up at them. 'Or would you like a double? We have one available.'

They blustered similar versions of, 'NO! Um ... no,' and then stood frowning in the awkward silence.

The receptionist gave a defensive shrug. 'Just trying to be helpful.'

Maggie eyed her, taking in her sulky pout. 'Thanks, but we booked two singles, and they'll do fine.'

The young woman sniffed and tossed two sets of keys onto the counter. 'The cabins are out the back. Dinner is available after six-thirty pm and breakfast from six am, in the beer garden.'

'Thanks.' Irked by the receptionist's petulance, Maggie said briskly, 'Do we need to book a table for dinner?'

'No, we're not full tonight, so you should be alright.'

'Great.' Maggie could feel Grayson staring at her. When they returned to the car to collect their gear she said, 'Sorry Gray, I should've checked with you first about dinner. If you'd prefer to eat alone—'

'Of course not. Does around seven suit you?'

'Fine.'

They made their way along a paved path to their adjoining cabins, located in a shady grove of trees a short walk from the main hotel building.

'Okay then, see you at seven.' Maggie unlocked her cabin and stepped inside. Someone had already turned on the air conditioner. It rattled away on the wall blowing refrigerated air into the stuffy cabin. Dropping her duffle onto one of the bunk beds, she went into the bathroom. It was tiny but clean and supplied with fresh, fluffy towels.

Eager for a cup of tea, followed by a shower to wash off the day's dust, she went back into the kitchen where she dug around in the cupboards and found tea bags and a mug. She filled the kettle and switched it on. While waiting for the water to boil, she opened her duffle and laid out fresh clothes and her toiletries bag. The kettle had just started to whistle when a knock came on the door. She rolled her eyes. Her tea would have to wait. Switching off the kettle, she went to the door.

Her eyes widened at the sight of Grayson standing on the narrow landing outside. Hunched over and dripping, he had a wet, rust-stained towel wrapped around his lower half and dirty water pooling around his bare feet. On hearing the door open, he raised his head and winked at her.

She stared at him, stunned. What the—?

Then she noticed suds and cloudy water running down his face and into his eyes. He wasn't winking, he was just trying to blink the stuff out.

He went to speak but had to spit out suds first before saying in a rush, 'Look, I'm sorry about this. While I was in the shower, the water pipes started hammering like you wouldn't believe, and then water and filthy muck,' and he pulled a face, 'exploded from the taps. I tried turning the water off and on again, but only got covered in more gunk. The same crap was gushing out of the kitchen tap as well, so I grabbed my mobile and tried to call reception, but couldn't raise anyone, and....' He glanced down at himself and then back at her, wincing. 'I can't exactly walk over there like this.'

He looked wretched, standing there covered in a slimy combination of soap suds and what looked like the contents of a decades-old grease trap, holding his towel closed with one hand and clutching a clean set of clothes in the other. Maggie's heart went out to him. All the same, mirth bubbled in her throat. Taking care to swallow it, she stepped back and motioned for him to follow her inside.

'Sure, use my bathroom. The water's okay here ... I think.' When she rushed to the bathroom vanity and turned on a tap, clean water gushed obligingly from the faucet. She nodded at him and moved back into the kitchen. 'All yours. Go on in.'

His sheepish look was spoiled when suds dripped into his eyes again, making him blink. 'Thanks. I know it's difficult ... in the circumst—' He paused, blinking, and squinted at her through one eye. 'I wouldn't impose only—'

'Don't worry about it, it's no big deal. Go ahead, I'll just ... um ... finish making my cuppa and have it out on the landing.'

'Well, thanks again. I won't be long.' He went in and closed the bathroom door.

Her eyes widened and she breathed, 'Wow,' while trying not to dwell on the image of his smooth, round pectorals and firm stomach above the towel. Sucking in a deep breath, she lifted her chin and hurried to finish making her tea, humming to blot out the sounds of Grayson showering just a thin partition away. As soon as it was ready, she took her steaming cup onto the landing. Closing the door behind her she lent against it, squeezing her eyes tightly closed and letting her head sag back until it bumped against the painted veneer.

So much for keeping our distance. I not only have a dinner date with Grayson, I'm also sharing my bathroom with him! First Harry, and now the plumbing. Is the universe conspiring to throw us together?

10

The only patrons in the hotel's public bar were a few dreary looking 'bar flies' – men in sweat-stained singlets and oily pants, some bare-footed, others with rubber thongs on grimy, calloused feet. They sat hunched over smeary beer glasses and only moved when Grayson and Maggie walked into the dimly lit, low-ceilinged room.

Seeing everyone turn to stare at them, Grayson bent his head to murmur, 'I guess they don't get many visitors up here.'

Maggie gave an impish grin and whispered, 'Yeah? What makes you say that?'

'Just a hunch.' He winked at her.

She swallowed the grin and moved forward, leaving a whiff of green apple shampoo hanging on the dusty air. She had left her hair loose to dry and it bounced in glossy waves around her shoulders and freshly scrubbed face. He allowed his gaze to linger, admiring the pale pink of her polo shirt against the soft bronze of her skin, and the way her boot-cut jeans hugged her lower body to the tops of her tan work boots.

Dragging his gaze away, he noticed the bar flies ogling her and shot them a narrow-eyed glance as if to say, *she's off limits,* at the same time reminding himself, *and don't YOU forget it either.*

The bartender bustled over, wiping grubby hands on an even grubbier tea towel and flicking aside a greasy lock of hair with a finger. 'What can I getcha, mate?'

While Grayson ordered their drinks, Maggie wandered the room to examine the dust and cobweb-daubed collection of framed black and white photos adorning the hotel's age-grimed walls. Most featured the establishment in its heyday, with large groups of grinning patrons spilling onto the veranda from the lounge bar or hanging over the upstairs railings. Some of the images were of formal functions, where it appeared the whole town had turned out in their Sunday best.

The township was more lively back then, she decided. Now it just felt heat-weary and sort of fed-up.

Returning to the bar, Maggie found Grayson leaning against it making small talk with the barman. Dressed in chinos and a pale, short-sleeved shirt, Grayson looked right at home in the country pub, if much better dressed than the other patrons. Leaning on both elbows pulled his shirt-sleeves taut, highlighting the muscle definition of his strong, tan arms. She whipped her gaze away, thankful she hadn't stayed in the cabin while he showered. She'd already glimpsed more of his physique than was wise, and the mental image of him stripped down to towel and soap suds, all muscles and masculinity, simply didn't bear thinking about. Even inhaling the steam that lingered after his hot shower had left her with a nagging feeling of guilt....

Turning from the bar, Grayson handed her a glass of 'house' white wine. It was full to the brim as though the barman had poured it like a beer. How many standard drinks did the large glass hold, she wondered. More than one, that's for sure.

What the heck, I'm not driving anywhere.

She took a sip. 'Hey, that's a nice sauv blanc!' She threw Grayson a rueful glance. 'I was thinking my choices would be a "chateau cardboard" chardonnay, or nothing.'

He twitched a dark eyebrow. 'And they don't skimp on their portions either. Want to head to the beer garden?' At her nod he led the way to the open-air dining area, where they sat at a table close to the sparse, tired-looking garden bed lining the walled courtyard. The overhanging fronds of a nearby palm swayed lazily above them in the warm evening breeze, revealing occasional glimpses of stars in the blackness of the outback night sky.

At the next table, a thirty-something couple sat gazing into a laptop's screen. The woman looked over at them and smiled. 'Hello there.'

'Hi.' Maggie smiled in return.

'I'm Cheryl and this is Gavin.'

'Maggie.'

'And I'm Grayson.' He leaned across to shake Gavin's hand. 'Where are you from?'

'The UK.'

'We're on a trip around Australia.' Cheryl inclined her head to indicate the laptop. 'Just updating our travel blog.'

Grayson nodded. 'I thought you sounded British. So, which part of the UK?'

When they launched into a discussion about places they knew in England, Maggie leaned back and let the conversation flow around her. She cradled her glass in both hands, sipping the wine and lingering over each fresh, grassy mouthful. She could feel herself mellowing thanks to the wine, balmy evening, pleasant company, and soft jazz music floating from speakers on the hotel's walls.

A waitress emerged to wander between the tables, distributing lit tea lights in small glass holders and taking meal orders as she went. Maggie opted for a char-grilled porterhouse steak and salad, while Grayson ordered the day's special, local-caught barramundi and chips.

'After all,' he pronounced, taking another swig from his frosty beer glass, 'when in Rome, one eats the pasta.'

The waitress beamed at him. 'You've made a good choice. We just got our seafood order today, so you're in for a treat.'

'Great.'

'Oh, and there's another treat in store for you all,' she added proudly, raising her voice so everyone could hear. 'You've heard of Kenny G, the famous sax player?' As she scanned the tables, heads nodded and there were murmurs of, 'Yeah,' and, 'Of course'.

'Well, Benny G is Burketown's answer to Kenny G, and he'll be playing for your musical pleasure later tonight. We'll clear a spot out here so you couples can get all cosy-dancey.'

'Oh, super!' Gavin and Cheryl were clearly thrilled at the prospect, while Maggie and Grayson nodded politely and sipped their drinks.

Gavin turned to them with a broad grin. 'This trip has become something of a second honeymoon for us. It's been *terrific*.'

Maggie gave an indulgent smile. 'How long have you been married?'

'About three years now,' Cheryl replied.

'Three years of wedded bliss!' Gavin gave his wife a one-armed hug and then turned to Grayson. 'And what about you two? How long have you been married?'

Maggie froze while Grayson said tightly, 'Oh! Um ... no ... we're not—'

'No need to be ashamed, man!' Gavin reached over to clap him on the back. 'You're together, that's all that counts. *We* waited ages before taking the plunge, didn't we love?'

Cheryl obliged with a nod.

'We really only did it 'cos we want to have a family one day,' Gavin continued. 'A marriage certificate is only a bit of paper after all, it doesn't prove how you feel about each other.' He beamed at Grayson. 'Even Blind Freddy could see you two are in love.'

Maggie's sudden splutter sprayed wine over the nearby garden bed. Coughing violently, she covered her face with her hands while Grayson swallowed a wry grin and thumped her on the back.

Cheryl raised incredulous eyebrows at her husband, who exclaimed, 'Oh, sorry! Did I say something wrong?'

'It's nothing.' Grayson gave Maggie's back another thump. 'It's just ... we're not a couple, just work colleagues.'

Gavin gave a disbelieving frown. 'You're kidding, right?' His eyes widened at Grayson's decisive headshake. 'Well, you could've fooled me.'

'Oh, crikey!' Cheryl's hand flew to her mouth as she watched the red-faced Maggie wave away Grayson's ministrations while succumbing to another coughing fit. 'I'm *so* sorry. I'm afraid Gavin has a bad case of foot-in-mouth disease when he gets overexcited. Just as well he married a lawyer, hey?' They shared an embarrassed titter.

To ease the awkward moment, Grayson assumed an exaggerated air of regret. 'Yes ... well ... I'm afraid my bliss years are still in front of me, unlike the rest of you "bliss-ters".' This time the laughter was genuine. 'Now, what were we talking about before? Oh yes, the traffic in Piccadilly Square. Man, that place is something else....'

Silently thanking him for smoothing over the *faux pas,* Maggie excused herself and hurried to the bathroom where she blew her nose, washed her face, dabbed the wine splatters from her clothes, and took a few minutes to regain her composure. She returned to the table to find their meals had been served. As she took her seat, Grayson glanced at her with mild amusement while on the other table, Cheryl and Gavin acknowledged her with apologetic nods as they tucked into their food. With a tight *yeah, you can laugh* smile at Grayson, Maggie sipped her wine, making sure to swallow it this time.

Her mouth watered when a warm aroma of char-grilled beef wafted up from her plate. When she took to the steak with her knife and fork she found it tender and cooked medium-well done, just as she'd ordered. The fresh mushroom sauce accompanying it was made with real cream, and the golden kumara mash beneath the steak held a delicate sweetness that accentuated the tanginess of the crisp side salad.

Judging by the silence at the two tables, broken only by the clatter of cutlery and murmurs of 'mm-mmm,' she knew she wasn't alone in enjoying her meal. Between mouthfuls she glanced up and found Grayson's eyes on her.

To conceal her discomfort at his silent scrutiny, she asked brightly, 'How do you like the north-western barramundi? Does it live up to your expectations?'

'It does indeed.' He dropped his gaze to the plate in front of him. 'I can't believe the size of this fillet. Like I said before, they're generous with their portions here.'

They had finished their meals and were refusing the waitress's offer of dessert when Benny G appeared. Of indeterminate age, he was dressed in an oversized t-shirt and baggy pants and carried a music case in one hand, music stand in the other, and more gear under his arms. It didn't take him long to set up in a corner of the courtyard, and after settling himself on a stool he pulled the microphone close.

'Evening folks. I'm Benny G, and this is a number from my namesake and idol, the late, great, *other* Benny G!' Putting a gleaming saxophone to his lips, he set off the backing track and launched with well-rehearsed confidence into a well-known Benny Goodman piece.

There were low chuckles and some muffled clapping from the diners. The gentle blues and jazz music flowed around the courtyard as if borne on a light breeze. Combined with the soft lighting and the warm night air, it gave the evening a memorable quality.

As Benny tilted his sax upward in a melodious finale, Maggie yawned. Maybe it was time to retire to her cabin....

Lowering his sax again Benny announced, 'Okay all you lovers, this one's for you. I wanna see you all up here, dancing your little hearts out!'

At the first strains of the romantic ballad, *The Way You Look Tonight,* Cheryl and Gavin rose to their feet. 'Oh yes, this is a great song.' Gavin waved a beckoning hand at Maggie and Grayson. 'C'mon guys, you heard the man. Let's get cosy-dancey.' Winding their arms around each other, they slid into a slow turn on the makeshift dance floor, swaying in time to the music.

When they paused in front of the table, again motioning for Grayson and Maggie to join them, Grayson raised a hand and shook his head. 'Thanks guys, but I think we'll sit this one out.'

Maggie breathed a sigh of relief and tried to ignore her

heart, which was doing its own version of the 'bad girl boogie'. Watching the dancers, she could see Gavin singing along with the music as he guided Cheryl around the small space.

Maggie took another mouthful of her wine.

'I see you've taken to *drinking* it now, instead of watering the garden with it?' Grayson raised a teasing eyebrow at her.

She swallowed and gave a rueful nod.

Gavin's voice drifted across to them. '... 'cos I *love* you ....'

Maggie gazed studiously into her wine glass, and then put it to her lips and drained it. 'Think I'll call it a night.' She rose a little unsteadily to her feet.

'I'll walk you to your cabin.'

'No need, I know the way. You stay and enjoy the evening.'

Grayson was already standing. 'I'm going to turn in as well.' As they made to leave, he waved goodnight to Cheryl and Gavin.

Maggie cringed when she saw Gavin give a huge wink, recalling with a sinking feeling his earlier words, 'Even Blind Freddy could see you two are in love....'

'That was a nice evening.' Grayson's voice sounded deeper in the heavy night air.

'Yes, and Gavin and Cheryl were ... friendly.'

He chuckled. 'An interesting couple. The meals were good too, don't you think?'

'Oh yes.'

They walked in silence the rest of the way to their cabins, and he waited on the path while Maggie unlocked her door. When she turned to wish him goodnight, the sight of him standing under the soft overhead lighting, so tall and strong and noble as he waited until she was safely inside, rendered her speechless. Their eyes met and her stomach took a nose-dive but she couldn't look away. They stared at each other for a long moment.

Finally, with a quiet, 'Goodnight Maggie,' he made his way to his own cabin.

His voice's warm resonance followed her inside.

Sleep did not come easily to her that night.

Despite a broken night's sleep, Maggie woke early and decided to slip out for breakfast on her own. When she got to the beer garden she found Grayson already there, chatting with a work crew who looked ready to head to a job site. She ran her eyes over the rough-looking bunch. It was hard to tell the women from the men. They were all dressed in the same high-vis work gear, had cigarettes tucked behind their ears, and swore loudly and often. It was a road crew, alright.

She took a seat at a table as a waitress emerged from inside the hotel, carrying a large carton bulging with cut sandwiches, biscuits, fruit, and thermos flasks. After dropping the box on the workers' table, the waitress began clearing the remnants of what looked to have been sizeable hot breakfasts.

Maggie smiled to herself. A big lunch after a big breakfast. Food certainly gained importance when work crews were out on site.

'Good morning.' Grayson pulled up a chair at her table. He obviously felt it was perfectly natural for them to eat together.

I wish he'd stayed where he was. Things get complicated when he's around....

From the wall-mounted speakers, a loud squawk interrupted the morning radio chatter. Movement in the garden ceased as all ears tuned to the emergency broadcast. Even the waitress stopped what she was doing to stand with her hands full of greasy, egg-smeared plates. At the conclusion of the broadcast she hurried inside, to emerge a few moments later loaded with more breakfast dishes.

As she put a plate of bacon and eggs in front of him, Grayson frowned across at Maggie. 'What does that cyclone warning mean for us?'

'Probably nothing.' Maggie nodded her thanks to the waitress, who finished delivering her continental breakfast and then scurried back to the kitchen. 'The warning is for coastal areas. Cyclones rarely make it this far inland. We might get some rain from it, though.' Her brow creased. 'This one's a biggie, by the sounds of it. I don't think Queensland's had a category five cyclone before.'

'Should we contact home base to check?'

'Might be a good idea.'

Grayson nodded. 'I'll get on the car two-way soon as I've finished eating.'

. . .

Maggie had just put the last spoonful of muesli into her mouth when he returned. Striding up to the table, he put his hands on the back of a chair and stood, head bent, staring thoughtfully at the ground.

'Did you get hold of them?'

He raised his eyes to fix her with a serious gaze. 'Harry's actually quite concerned about this cyclone's severity. He says it's been growing in size and intensity since forming in the Pacific, and is making a beeline for the North Queensland coast.'

'Oh no!' She paused to chew her lip. 'They don't think it's any threat to us out here, though?'

'Not directly. It's the coastal cities that are most at risk. According to Harry, people there are battening down the hatches in preparation for a "big blow" – the largest cyclone Queensland has encountered, apparently. That said, he wants us to return to Cloncurry, just in case.'

She sat back heavily. 'Damn, after coming all this way! I'll have to cut short the code of conduct sessions I'd planned to give the gulf crew.'

'That's a shame, Maggie. I know you wanted to spend time working through it with them.'

Her frown deepened. 'I was particularly keen to do one-on-one sessions with a few of the guys. It's the main reason I came up here.'

'Harry knew you'd be disappointed but said it'll simply

have to wait. He doesn't think we'll get the storm itself, but he *is* worried about the possibility of flash flooding stranding us on the road. So he wants us to leave here by tomorrow at the latest.'

She heaved a sigh. 'Oh well, he's the boss. And I guess that still leaves us with today, so it's not a completely wasted trip.' She got to her feet. 'Guess we'd better make the most of the time we have.'

'Before we go, I need to report the plumbing problem in my cabin.'

She nodded. 'While we're at reception I'll cancel our third night's accommodation.'

The bored-looking receptionist, whose name badge identified him as 'Slobodan', noted the change in their booking. Then, while Grayson spoke to him, Maggie glanced at the TV mounted above the reception counter. Plastered across the screen a satellite image showed the huge storm making its destructive way toward the coast.

She sucked in a breath. 'Oh no ... it's enormous, nearly the size of the whole state! And it's almost on top of Cairns.' She turned to fix the men with anxious eyes. 'I thought the earlier report said it was expected to turn south before it crossed the coast.'

They peered at the screen and Slobodan muttered ominously, 'Yeah, well these cyclones have minds of their own, it's no wonder they give 'em girl's names. There won't be much left of the city once that mean cow's had 'er way with it.'

Grayson put a comforting hand on Maggie's arm. 'I'm

sure they're prepared for this. Cyclones are regular occurrences in the state's north, aren't they?'

'Yes, but look at the *size* of this one!'

They stared at the TV screen until he nudged her gently. 'C'mon Maggie, we'd better get going.'

She nodded and followed him out, after a final apprehensive look at the image of the super storm bearing down on tropical North Queensland's capital city.

Later, as they travelled to the job site, the car's AM/FM radio once again crackled and died.

Grayson flicked her a glance. 'That's it for the cyclone updates I guess.'

''Til we get back this evening.' Maggie's eyes filled with foreboding. 'Will Cairns still be standing by then? And its rainforest surrounds and famous barrier reef?' She turned away, giving one side of her face a nervous rub. 'Or will it have been obliterated by this monster storm?'

It was a quiet trip, though not an awkward silence this time. Absorbed in their own thoughts, they occasionally squinted at the sky as though looking for signs of approaching danger, and shared the odd worried glance.

They arrived at the work site in good time to be greeted by the project supervisor, Trevor, a stocky older man with a gravelly voice. His craggy, weathered face broke into a smile when Maggie shook his hand. Rasping, 'Got the guys assembled ready for ya,' he indicated where his crew sat in a rough circle under the shade of a tree, smoking and talking among themselves.

She nodded her thanks, gathered her training materials, and strode over to the group. It was time to push aside all other thoughts and concentrate on relaying the most important information. She glanced down at her materials, hoping the cut-down version she'd hastily prepared would do the job, and help the workmen keep theirs. They watched her approach with open curiosity. Hopefully they'd be receptive....

Grayson turned to Trevor. 'Ready to go?'

'Yup.'

The two men made their way to a waiting job truck, climbed into the cab, kicked the big diesel engine into life, and commenced a crawling inspection of the roadworks.

They returned some time later. Grayson jumped down from the truck and jogged toward where Maggie stood to the side of the group. She was talking quietly with one of the men.

'... so you see, Rocky, it's important we all present a professional image to the motoring public, even when they don't return the courtesy. And we're not only doing it for them, but for us as well. We all want to keep our jobs.'

Grayson waited for a break in the conversation and then stepped in to tap her on the shoulder.

She turned to him with raised eyebrows. 'You've finished your inspection *already*?'

His reply was blunt. 'We had to cut it short. A message

came through on the two-way for this crew to pull up digs and head back. *Now.*'

'Oh no! The cyclone?'

Seeing her eyes widen with alarm, Grayson suppressed the urge to put a comforting arm around her. 'Yes,' he said gruffly, 'it's crossed the coast—'

'Cairns?' Her voice was breathless with urgency.

'Safe.'

She exhaled. 'Oh ... thank goodness.'

Trevor sauntered up to join them, saying glumly, 'The towns south of it didn't do so well, but. The cyclone crossed the coast 'tween Cairns and Townsville, which was a blessing for them cities ... not for the small towns in between.'

All three shook their heads and exhaled.

'Anyway,' Trevor went on, 'the cyclone didn't weaken as much as expected after it hit the coast. It's headin' straight for us, still as a category four.' Catching his 2IC's eye, he signalled for the men to begin packing up the camp.

Maggie gaped at him. 'Are you saying it's now threatening the inland region?'

Already striding away, he called over a shoulder, 'That's right,' and made for where the crew was rousing. 'And it's cuttin' a swathe through the countryside as it travels. It'll probably lose intensity fairly quickly now it's over land. All the same, I'd get packin' if I was you. Crews don't get called off a job for nothin'.'

Feeling Grayson's hand on her arm, Maggie turned to him with downcast eyes. 'Well ... at least I accomplished a *bit* of what I came all this way to do.'

He patted her arm. 'C'mon love, let's go.'

They made their way to the car while the work crew scurried around them, making swift work of gathering their equipment and dismantling the site. At the rate they were going, they'd be hard on the heels of their light-travelling guests.

Grayson nosed the vehicle to where Trevor was directing his crew's efforts. 'We're off now. Will we see you back in Burketown?'

Trevor shook his head. 'Nah, we're headin' straight to the Curry.'

'Is that a good idea? I thought these roads were best left to the beasts at night?'

'Yeah, but I reckon the circumstances warrant it this time. I have a bunch of guys here keen to get home to their families, they'll be happy to share the drivin'. 'N this big job truck can handle anythin' that gets in our way,' and he slapped the solid metal bull bar protecting the front of the truck.

Grayson turned to Maggie. 'Do you think we should tag along with them?'

A frown creased her brow.

Do we risk travelling the road at night, or wait 'til the morning and risk being stranded by flash flooding?

She looked through the car's window at the cloudless blue of the afternoon sky, and felt a warm breeze caress her cheek. It seemed inconceivable that a deadly storm was heading their way. Surely they'd have time to get home safely if they left first thing in the morning?

When she looked back at him, still uncertain, Grayson

turned to Trevor. 'Think we'll be heading off first thing tomorrow. Safe travels chaps, take it easy on the highway. Remember, the most important thing is to get home safely.'

Wishing them a safe journey in return, Trevor gave the bonnet of their car a farewell thump before bellowing at his crew, 'Better get crackin', boys.'

11

Grayson sat at ease in the driver's seat, right elbow on the arm rest and left hand gripping the steering wheel while he stared at the road ahead, watchful for potholes and straying beasts. Beside him Maggie gazed out the window absorbed in her thoughts as the red dirt country-side and its sparse, grey vegetation sped past.

Troy.

She gave a start.

In all that had happened, she hadn't given her husband a moment's consideration! Hadn't contacted him, hadn't even *thought* about him until now.

How could he have slipped her mind? Considering the situation she was in, shouldn't she have a need to reach out to her 'other half' for reassurance?

She flicked Grayson a sideways glance. It was true he made her feel safe, and ... complete somehow, but....

He's not my husband, Troy is.

She chewed her lower lip.

Get a grip, get a grip, get a grip.

She took a deep breath.

I'll phone home as soon as I have mobile reception again.

That silent pledge helped ease her conscience ... a bit.

As the lights of Burketown began to blink on the horizon, discernible sounds issued from the car's radio. When Grayson reached across to turn it up, she said, 'Gray, I think I'll be after an early night when we get back.'

The purposeful steeliness in his eyes softened the instant they fell on her face. 'Probably a good idea. We'll need to make an early start in the morning ... at first light if you're up for it?'

She nodded.

A moment later the *weeeoo, weeeoo, weeeoo* siren of a cyclone warning wailed from the speakers. Grayson increased the volume so they could hear the update. As the announcer's carefully dispassionate voice warned of a continued storm threat, Maggie sank further in her seat. She felt thoroughly bone-weary. It was all too much; the looming cyclone, having to cut short the training session that was the whole reason for the trip, the prospect of a long, tiring journey ahead, and the constant nagging guilt about Troy. Her nerves felt stretched to breaking.

She rubbed a hand across her forehead.

Not far now....

.　.　.

Back at the hotel, Grayson slipped away while she was unloading her gear from the car. He returned a few minutes later and announced, 'I've ordered dinner to be delivered to our cabins, hope that's okay with you? I figured you'd want to eat in.'

She stood with her heavy laptop bag weighing down a shoulder, hands full of folders with other training gear piled on top of them, and threw him a grateful smile. 'Thanks.' Sighing, she lifted her free shoulder and wiped her head against it to remove the perspiration from under her eyes and nose. It left a damp, dusty mark on her blouse. 'That's thoughtful of you.'

Noticing her pallor under the smudges of dust, he took the laptop bag and bulkiest folders from her. 'Don't mention it. I just hope you like what I've ordered for you.'

She gave another wan smile. 'I'm sure I will,' and with her free hand, fished out the keys to her cabin.

After they made their way along the path, Grayson followed her inside her cabin to drop the gear on the table. As she turned to thank him, Maggie was hit by an attack of dizziness. She wobbled against the table and gripped its edge, blinking in an effort to clear the cotton wool filling her head. Still it felt like the room was shrinking around her, the walls closing in.

Nausea rose within her.

She bent her head and squeezed her eyes closed, willing her equilibrium to return.

'Are you alright, Maggie?'

She felt Grayson put a steadying hand on her elbow.

When she dared to open her eyes, she found him gazing down at her with concern. She swayed toward him as though drawn by a magnetic force.

He's so close, and so caring, and I could *so* use a hug....

'Maggie?'

His voice sounded husky and oddly distant, considering their closeness. When he grasped her upper arms, his hands were warm, strong, and gentle.

She swallowed hard and straightened. 'I'm ... okay.' To her own ears her voice sounded hollow. 'Just ... a little worn out I guess.' She rubbed her eyes and gave a weak smile.

He peered into her face with a worried frown. 'Are you sure you're alright?' The gentle concern in his voice brought to mind an image of honey dripping from a hot buttered crumpet. Lovely ... but perilous to the willpower. She nodded without speaking and bent her head again.

This is all too much. I'm *miles* from home with a man I should – but can't – regard as simply another work colleague, and the whole purpose of this damn trip has been blown away by a monster of a cyclone that's now bearing down on us, and I'm feeling more and more like death warmed up, and although all I'd have to do is lean a bit his way to be wrapped in comfort ... I can't accept it.

She stifled a sob, squeezed her eyes tightly shut again, and wished herself miles away ... while also desperate to stay right where she was, in Grayson's comforting presence.

'Maggie?' When she didn't answer, he put a hand under her chin to tip her face upward. Seeing the tears welling in her eyes, he breathed, 'Oh Maggie, love,' and wrapped his arms around her. 'Don't cry.'

All her resolutions evaporated as she sagged against his broad chest. With her ear close to his heart and feeling its strong beats reverberating through her own body, one certainty emerged.

Something that feels this right can't be wrong. And it doesn't just feel right, it also feels safe, and comforting. And even if it *is* wrong, for a minute – just this one precious minute – I don't care.

She allowed herself to relish his embrace before summoning her strength and drawing away. He loosened his hold but kept his hands on her arms to steady her.

'I'm ... sorry about that, Gray.' Her mouth felt numb and her tongue stumbled over the words. Her brow creased and she gave a small, self-conscious chuckle. 'Guess I just needed a hug. It's been a long day.'

When he once more tipped her face to gaze into her eyes, she managed to look at him with a semblance of normality. Giving a small nod, he let her go and took a step back, saying stiffly, 'Glad I could help,' adding as much for his own benefit as for hers, 'someone had to stand in for Troy.'

And suddenly there were three of them in the tiny cabin.

Although Troy's was an invisible presence, to Maggie's ragged emotions the room felt crowded and even more oppressive than before. And as Grayson made to leave, she felt the circle of comfort she'd enjoyed for that short time go with him, leaving her standing unprotected in the aching harshness of reality.

At the door he half-turned to gaze searchingly at her for another long moment, before dipping his head in a curt nod and walking out. As the door closed behind him, she took two faltering steps to the bed, collapsed onto it, and gave in to the tears.

Dawn was nudging the dark edges of the horizon the following morning when Grayson knocked quietly on Maggie's door. He stepped down from the landing and listened. It was earlier than they'd arranged and he half expected her to be still asleep, so was surprised when the door opened and light spilled onto the path, making him squint.

Maggie stepped onto the landing, fully dressed, bulging duffle in her hand. She dropped it on the floor and locked the cabin.

When she turned to look at him, he nodded his approval. 'Ready to go?'

'Sure am.' She bent to collect her bag, thinking their voices sounded brittle in the stillness of the early morning air.

Brittle ... and stilted, as if their closeness the evening before had pushed them further apart.

As she came down the steps Grayson took the heavy bag from her, and when they got to the car he put it in the back beside his.

'You've been down here already?' She kept her voice low in deference to the time of day.

'I woke early.'

'Oh.'

Maybe he didn't sleep well either....

After they'd settled themselves in the front seats and closed the doors, the silence in the cabin and his proximity got the better of her. With forced brightness she blustered, 'Gray, I must apologise ... about last night—'

'No need to apologise, you were tired. We both were.'

Their eyes met across the car's cabin and they shared a cautious smile that said nothing ... and everything.

Grayson turned the key in the ignition and said matter-of-factly, 'It's too early to order a sit-down breakfast, so I arranged a take-away. Hope that's okay with you? I was thinking we could stop at one of the picnic spots along the Gregory River to have it.'

'Mm. Breakfast by the river sounds nice.'

'Okay. Well, if you're set, we'll hit the road.'

She nodded as he put the car in gear and nosed it out. Within minutes they were on the open highway, where she watched the landscape emerge from beneath night's thick, dark quilt. They had their windows rolled down, savouring the morning's cool freshness while it lasted, and she was grateful for the rushing air. Its noise helped fill the awkward conversational void between them, a silence Grayson didn't seem inclined to break any time soon.

She sighed.

May as well grab some shut-eye.

Reaching behind to take the rug from the back seat, she folded it beneath her head, crossed her arms, and leaned against the car door.

Grayson sat in the driver's seat, hands gripping the wheel, eyes fixed on the road ahead, pondering the correlation of the past with the present.

Had Tina and lover boy Nolan enjoyed little trips away together, like this? Of course theirs would've been to exotic destinations, knowing Tina's fondness for the good life. All the same, he could imagine them sneaking away during his work trips, travelling hip-to-hip in a car's close confines, Nolan's hand on her leg as she snuggled against him, her coquettish smile full of promise....

His voice was gruff when he broke the silence, jolting Maggie out of a doze. 'There's a spot ahead that might be suitable.'

She yawned and sat up. 'Great.' Some food to settle her empty and increasingly querulous stomach would be welcome.

Grayson slowed and pulled off the road, nosing the car under the shade of a tree beside a sparse patch of grass. The rising sun was gilding everything with its radiant touch, so shade was called for despite the early hour.

Turning off the ignition, he got out and opened the back door.

'Want this?'

Maggie held out the blanket and he took it from her,

spreading it over the grassed area beneath the tree. Then he collected a box containing thermos, paper cups, the makings of tea, two buttered fruit buns and some fresh fruit. Maggie found herself smiling at the prospect of breakfast by the gently gurgling river.

He glanced over, caught her smile, and gave a slow grin. 'You're hungry too, hey?'

'You bet!'

Just a small exchange of words, but with it the atmosphere between them eased.

She knelt on the rug and made their tea while he laid out the rest of the spread. After filling their plates, they found comfy spots leaning against the trunk of the shade tree and ate their breakfast in companionable silence.

Slapping his hands together to dislodge any lingering crumbs, Grayson gazed at the cloudless sky. 'You wouldn't think there's a storm coming this way, would you?'

Maggie shook her head and said briskly, 'No, but there is.' She popped the last morsel of bun into her mouth and got to her feet. Grayson rose too, and in soundless agreement they packed up the breakfast things and got underway again.

Once up at highway speed, he pressed the button on the car's CD player and music filled the cabin. They were a few songs in when he spotted a car on the side of the road ahead.

'I wonder if someone's in trouble.'

At his words Maggie peered ahead, trying to see if anyone was with the car, while Grayson eased his pressure on the accelerator and the engine revs immediately decreased. Tom had told him that people needed a good reason to pull over in the outback, so it was always wise to check. Seeing the other vehicle's occupants emerge to wave them down, he slowed further and drew alongside their car.

When a middle-aged indigenous man approached the driver's side, Grayson rolled down the window and the man leaned in. He was quickly surrounded by two young children and a teenager. Near the other car a woman lay on the ground and another knelt beside her, fanning her with a piece of cardboard.

'Ay mate, glad you come by.' His voice was raspy and hard to hear, and he avoided making direct eye contact.

'Hello. What's up?'

'Me missus, she be sick, ay?'

Maggie opened her door. 'I'll check on her.'

Grayson waited until she was clear before moving off and parking in front of the other vehicle. He got out, running his eyes over the dusty old Holden station wagon. Its paint was faded and peeling, all the hub caps were missing, and there were few – if any – straight panels.

He strode back to where the others stood watching him. 'What's with your car?'

''Im not workin' no more. Look 'ere,' and the man pointed a bony finger at the missing petrol cap.

'Ah. You've run out of fuel?'

The man nodded.

From where she knelt beside the prone woman, Maggie looked up to ask, 'What's your name?'

'Billy.'

'What's wrong with your wife, Billy?'

'She got the diabetic.'

'Does she need insulin?'

'Yeah.'

'Do you have some?'

'Nah, used it all last night. We was goin' to get some from da Isa, but...,' and he shrugged his skinny shoulders.

Rising, Maggie motioned for Grayson to join her and they moved out of earshot.

When he commented, 'I found it a bit hard to grasp what Billy was saying,' she said, 'We're actually lucky they speak such good English,' and glanced at them thoughtfully. 'I think this family is from the coast. Most indigenous folk out here speak a creole, which is a lot harder to understand.' When her eyes found the prone woman again, she frowned. 'Gray, she doesn't look in good shape. She's lethargic and disoriented, and feels awfully hot, so is probably running a temperature. She must be way overdue for an insulin injection. We have to do something.'

'What? We can't take them all in the car with us, there's not enough room.'

'The two-way still has reception, doesn't it?'

He nodded.

'Then we'd better call the Flying Doctors.'

'Oh, right! The outback's version of "Dial-a-Doctor".'

'Yes. Hopefully they'll be able to come and get her, or at least bring some insulin for her. And maybe a jerry can of petrol. Unless our spare fuel...?'

'Diesel. No good in their petrol guzzler.' He glanced back

at their fleet vehicle. 'If radioing doesn't work I'll use the emergency position indicating radio beacon.'

'Oh, you brought an EPIRB along? That was good thinking.'

'We might not need to use it. I'll try the radio first.' Striding to the car, he slid into the front seat and she heard him click the button on the two-way to select the emergency channel. Pressing the transmit button on the speaker mic he said clearly, 'Emergency, emergency, emergency. This is Main Roads vehicle two five six on the Wills Developmental Road, requesting urgent medical assistance.'

As Maggie returned to the prone woman's side, the others gathered around her. Looking down at the sick woman, she said gently, 'My name's Maggie, what's yours?'

Stretching up a weak, shaking hand, the woman rasped, 'Rosie.'

Taking her hand, Maggie noted its clamminess. 'Rosie, we're sending for the Flying Doctor. You're going to be alright.'

Rosie's bloodshot eyes fluttered open again and she murmured through dry lips, 'Tank you, missus.'

'Are you sure you don't have any insulin in the car somewhere?'

'No missus, I use 'im all last night.'

It was obviously an effort for her to speak, so Maggie said gently, 'You rest, Rosie, we'll take care of you.' She turned to the others gathered around her. 'Won't we?' They gazed at her with trusting brown eyes and nodded solemnly.

Inside the fleet vehicle, Grayson clipped the radio mic

back on its hook and got out. Coming to stand at the edge of the group, he waited while Maggie gave the sick woman a drink of water and then gestured for her to join him. She studied his face for an indication of whether the news was good or bad. His expression was serious but otherwise gave nothing away.

As she reached his side he said quietly, 'The Flying Doctor will be a while. The plane's on another call-out and will have to get back to base and re-fuel first. Let's hope the weather holds.'

They glanced apprehensively at the sky. It was still blue and clear but with an ominous line of grey forming on the far eastern horizon.

Maggie murmured, 'Let's hope Rosie can hold on too.'

'Is that her name?'

'Mm.' Maggie gazed up at him. 'Can we do anything for her in the meantime, did they say?'

'Make her comfortable, keep her fluids up, and get her to that landing strip on the road to meet the plane.'

She exhaled and raked fingers through her hair. 'It doesn't seem like much. I feel a bit useless, really.'

'You and I both. But I'm sure *they're* glad we're here to help.' He inclined his head at the family and then said grimly, 'You know this will significantly delay our return to Cloncurry?'

'Yes.' She raised her hands in a helpless gesture. 'But what else can we do? They need our help.'

Nodding, he shaded his eyes and peered into the distance. 'Right, we'd better start the ferry service to the landing strip.' He lowered his gaze to give her an encouraging smile. 'It'll only take a couple of trips to get us all there.'

'Okay.'

'From memory, there's not much cover near the landing strip. Rosie's probably better off going with the second lot, and resting here in the shade until then.' Giving Maggie's hand a quick squeeze, he strode over to the others calling cheerily, 'All aboard! The outback express is leaving for the airport.'

Maggie watched him round up his relieved passengers, gratitude and pride swelling in her chest.

She glanced at her watch.

They'd been gone an hour, and there was no sign of another vehicle on the road that whole time.

Grayson hadn't been happy about leaving her behind, but when Billy, teenaged Seb and the other woman, Olive, who turned out to be Rosie's sister, were the first to jump in the car, Grayson had no choice but to leave Maggie there to look after Rosie and the children. So, after giving her the EPIRB and a generous supply of water, he climbed into the driver's seat and started the fleet vehicle.

When she rested a hand on the open car window and whispered, 'Come back as soon as you can,' he gave her hand a reassuring squeeze.

'Back before you know it.'

As she stood watching him drive off, she felt a small hand slip into hers and another wrap around her leg. Looking down, she saw the children pressing close to her, waving goodbye to their family members until the car became a small dot against the heat-shimmering horizon.

Maggie eyed Rosie anxiously. The sick woman lay quiet, probably fading in and out of consciousness. In between checking on her, Maggie played with the two children, glad of their lively company. As she sat idly watching them use gnarled twigs to draw pictures in the bull dust beside the road, it crossed her mind that they could all be doomed if Grayson didn't return for some reason. That was the nature of the outback – beautiful, untamed, and dangerous to the unwary or unlucky.

She gave in and looked at her watch again.

Ninety minutes since Grayson left and fifteen since the battered old farm truck went past. The equally battered-looking driver had slowed with a questioning glance at her and she'd waved him on, hoping she wasn't watching their salvation trundle away in a cloud of dust. They could've hitched a ride with him but what if along the way they missed seeing Grayson, or he didn't notice them waving for him to stop from the back of the truck? He'd arrive at the broken-down car as arranged only to find nobody there.

No, they had to stick with the plan and wait for him to return.

She checked on Rosie again, made sure the children

drank some water before having some herself, and then slumped against the shaded side of the old Holden. When, a short time later, she heard the distant sound of an approaching vehicle, her eyes snapped open. Praying they weren't about to be visited by an escaped axe murderer on the lookout for more hapless victims, she sat upright, just as the children called, 'Hey, missus! Look 'ere! Mister back.'

She jumped to her feet, shading her eyes with a hand, and peered down the road. Seeing the fleet vehicle approaching with Grayson at the wheel, she gave an audible sigh of relief.

He pulled in beside them and wound down the window. 'Everyone still okay?'

'Yes.' So much relief and gratitude in that one word. 'And very glad you're back.'

'Right then, let's load up again.' He opened his door and climbed down, leaving the motor running. Artificially cooled air rushed out after him and was immediately consumed by the heat. 'We need to get a move on, the plane might beat us there if we don't hurry.'

'Have you had an update?'

'They contacted me on the two-way, said the plane had made it to base and was re-fuelling for this trip.'

'Great news.' Smiling widely, Maggie called, 'C'mon kids, hop in the car. It's our turn now.'

After strapping the two chattering youngsters into the front passenger seat, Grayson came to where Maggie was helping Rosie to her feet. When the sick woman swayed and looked in danger of collapsing, he swung her into his arms and carried her to the car, where Maggie opened the door and spread the rug over the back seat. After he carefully laid Rosie on it, Maggie got in beside her and rested the sick woman's head in her lap.

Grayson gave her a nod and then slid into the driver's seat. 'Okay, we all ready?'

At the children's cries of, 'Yes Mister, let's go!' he once again guided the vehicle onto the road and accelerated away in a shower of gravel.

While Maggie strapped the children into their seats on the plane, Grayson stood outside having a word with the pilot. Rosie lay on a stretcher in the plane's aisle, covered in a fresh white sheet, having received medical attention on the airstrip just minutes after the Beechcraft touched down. She beckoned Maggie and tried to tell her something, but the plane's idling engines drowned out her weak voice.

Maggie took her outstretched hand. 'Shh, Rosie, you need to rest now.'

At a signal from his wife, Billy edged closer to Maggie. 'Hey, lady.'

'Yes, Billy?'

'My missus 'ere, she say you in danger. Big storm comin'.'

'Oh, is that what she was trying to tell me?'

'Yeah. She say, you go Black Mountain where her people been. You be high, you be safe.'

'Thanks, but I think we'll be coming on the plane with

you.' Maggie smiled at Rosie, thinking she already looked brighter.

'Maggie?'

She turned to see Grayson motioning for her to join him outside. The pilot climbed the airstairs after she stepped down them, and she watched him join the medic in the cockpit, no doubt to finish the pre-flight checks.

Leading her away from the plane's noisy twin-props, Grayson said, 'They need to take off soon. With the wild weather approaching they can't afford to delay.'

She nodded. 'So we'd better secure the car and get on board.'

'*You're* getting on board. *I'm* driving the car back.'

'But—'

'But nothing.' He gave her a push toward the air stairs.

'Hang on!' She dug in her heels. 'What about you? Don't tell me you're worried about the car, 'cos it can wait—'

'There's only one seat left on the plane,' he said tightly, 'yours.'

She frowned. '*One* seat? But surely an extra person won't make a difference?' Her expression brightened. 'I don't mind standing—'

He smiled crookedly at her and shook his head. 'With nine on board they're already risking being overweight. It's lucky two of the passengers are only little. Look, I'll be fine, Maggie, don't worry about me.'

'But I *am* worried. You won't make it to town before the storm hits.'

'So I'll drive until it's not safe to go on, and then find somewhere to shelter. I'm not completely useless you know.'

'I never said you were, but—'

'We have to go!' They turned to see the pilot standing at the top of the airstairs with one hand on the cable, ready to retract the stairs and close the hatch for take-off.

Grasping her elbow, Grayson marched her to the stairs. 'You're wasting time, Maggie. The plane has to leave.'

She fixed him with anxious eyes. 'Gray—' but he was already backing away.

Raising a hand in a smiling salute he called, 'Have a good trip. See you in the Curry.' With a cheery wave at the children in the plane, he strode to the car to prepare for what was now to be a solo journey.

While laying the folded blanket over the gear in the back, he heard the plane's engines roar and turned to see the Beechcraft charge along the makeshift runway. When it lifted into the afternoon sun he shaded his eyes with a hand, squinting as the plane climbed skyward and watching until it became a dark speck against the blue ... and was accosted by the same feeling of desertion he'd experienced in Heathrow's departure lounge.

When Tina turned her back on him, their marriage, and their future.

Another correlation between past and present....

Pushing those thoughts aside with an annoyed grunt, he spun on his heel and made his way to the front of the car.

And that's when he saw her.

12

Sitting with the passenger's seat tilted back, crossed ankles propped on the open door and a hat down over her face, it looked for all the world like she was dozing.

Grayson marched up to snatch away the hat and glare down at her. 'You're supposed to be safely on that plane,' and he stabbed a finger at the sky behind him. 'What the HELL are you doing still here?'

'I didn't feel much like a plane trip today,' Maggie said coolly. 'I get air sick, you know.'

He threw both hands in the air and swore.

'Now, now. There's no need for bad language.'

'This isn't funny.' He stared darkly at her. 'I want to know why you didn't go.'

She sighed, dropped her feet to the car's running board and sat upright to look him in the eye. 'Gray, there was no way under the northern sun I was going to simply fly off and leave you to face the storm alone. We came out here together, and that's how we're going home ... together.'

He was silent a moment, his face working, then he said, 'So you sneaked back to the car while I was busy organising the gear?'

'And watching the plane leave. Must say, that was a fond farewell you gave us ... er ... them.'

At her wiggle of brows his lips tightened. 'I told you I'd be fine, especially knowing you were safe.'

'Yeah, right. Like *you* know what to do in the middle of a cyclone in one of the most remote parts of Australia.'

'And you do?'

She sobered. 'Well, more of an idea than a born-'n-bred Brit would have.' When he scowled and turned away, she raised her voice a notch. 'I have a duty of care, after all, and I figure that between us we'll keep each other safe.' When this earned her an affronted glare she added quickly, 'Oh, I'm sure you can look after yourself.' Alighting from the car, she moved to stand in front of him, hands on hips. 'But I brought you out here, and by hook or by crook I'm going to take you back again, in one healthy piece.'

They stood in the dust facing each other, stubborn determination versus angry frustration, until the fire died in his eyes. Bending his head, he ran a hand over his close-cropped hair and sighed. 'Well, no point crying over spilt milk, or departed planes.' He raised his head again. 'C'mon, if we're in this together then let's get going.'

His gruff words masked the jumble of emotions he was experiencing. By choosing to stay with him, had she somehow dispersed the dark shadow cast over him by loneliness, regret, and self-reproach?

It sure felt that way.

With a new buoyancy to his step, he went to the driver's side, got in and started the motor.

She slid in beside him. 'Wait, Gray. Look at the sky.'

Leaning forward to peer through the windscreen, he saw dense, towering thunderheads closing in, swallowing the blue and blanketing the sun. He gave a long whistle. At her quiet, 'The storm's nearly here,' he put the car in gear and barked, 'And we're *out* of here. Buckle up.'

Over the noise of the car's tyres spinning in the roadside gravel as it bounced and lurched onto the bitumen, she said, 'Billy and Rosie knew a safe place to shelter from the storm. They said we should go to ... um....' She screwed up her face, recalling the scene on the plane. 'It was ... Black Mountain ... at Coolullah.' She opened her eyes again. 'Yep, that's it. Billy said something about driving to the end of the road and looking up. We're supposed to see a safe place.'

'Right then.' With a resolute nod, Grayson accelerated hard through the gears. 'It's Black Mountain or bust.'

By the time they reached the turn-off the countryside was shrouded in gloom under threatening steel-grey clouds. Grayson drove to the end of the corrugated gravel road and stopped with the motor idling to scan the area, looking for the 'safe place' Billy and Rosie had mentioned.

'Billy said to look up, right?'

'Mm.' Sweeping another glance over their surroundings she saw only sparse scrub country littered with rocks and boulders. And then.... 'Over there! That must be it.'

He followed her pointing finger to a rocky embankment with a dark opening halfway up the slope. 'Is that a cave?'

'Looks like it.'

'Well,' he said slowly, rubbing his lightly stubbled chin, 'it's certainly high enough to be out of reach of any flooding ... and those boulders around the outside form a sort of buttress.' He glanced at her. 'So I guess you've found the place.'

They shared a triumphant grin as he put the car into four-wheel drive and began inching it over the rough ground, heading for the base of the embankment. When he spotted a rugged path cut into the slope that appeared to lead to the cave's entrance, he braked and pointed to it.

'A bit overgrown but looks to have been well used, just not for a while. The cave's probably the same.'

She nodded.

Peering up at it, he said slowly, 'I don't think we should assume the cave is vacant.'

'We'll have to be careful.' She flicked him a significant glance. 'Who knows what we might disturb by going in there.'

Mumbling, 'What ... or who,' he unclipped his seatbelt and opened his door. The wind immediately rushed in, its temperature varying from scorching hot to strangely chilled. The sound of it howling and whipping through the surrounding vegetation filled the cabin. He had to raise his voice above the din. 'Right, after we've checked out the cave I'll scout around for somewhere sheltered to park the car.'

They made their way through scrubby growth to the base of the path and began climbing the rough-hewn steps. When they got to the cave's entrance he indicated for Maggie to stay outside while he ventured in. She watched him disappear into the gloom, wishing she'd thought to give him a torch, and then a light flashed on in the cave's interior.

Good for you, boy scout.

She gave a wry huff.

After all my brave talk about keeping him safe, I hope it's not me who ends up needing to be saved.

His voice emerged from within the cave. 'It's okay, you can come in.'

When she stepped inside she found him standing in the centre of a spacious, sandy and relatively clean area. When he focused the torch beam upward to illuminate the whole cavern, the light revealed the steep pitch of the cave's roof. It rose sharply from the entranceway so that even Grayson could move around without having to bend his head.

There were animal and other footprints in the sandy floor, and against the rocky wall, the remnants of a fireplace. She took an exploratory sniff of the air and found it earthy but fresh.

Grayson pointed to the back of the cavern where the ground flattened out. 'There's a good spot to spread the blanket.'

'Mm.' Eyeing the spot and deciding there was enough

room for them to stretch out there to sleep, her stomach sank to her toes.

Sleeping here.

Together.

Alone.

Clammy fingers of panic – and another sensation she refused to acknowledge – clawed at her insides. 'Gray ... um....' Her voice came out in a squeak. She swallowed, her expression pained. 'Are you sure we shouldn't just keep driving?'

'What?' He turned to her with a frown. 'Is something wrong?'

'No ... but ... I was wondering....' She fidgeted with her hair, her movements jerky, agitated.

He stared at her and then said, 'Maggie,' in a soothing but firm tone, 'the cyclone's almost upon us. If we'd kept driving we would have found ourselves in the middle of it. The last directive we received was to seek shelter and wait out the storm, and that's what we're doing.'

'Yes, I know, but—'

'And that directive came from Harry, our boss, who expects us to do what he says.'

She gnawed her bottom lip, doubt hovering in her eyes.

Cupping an ear with a hand, he said sharply, 'Hear that?'

She caught the rising howl of the wind past the cave entrance.

'It's getting worse.' He took a moment to prop the torch against the wall before going to the entrance. 'C'mon, we have to unload the car.'

As they emerged from behind the rocky buttress they were immediately buffeted by powerful wind gusts. In the sky above, the last skerrick of blue vanished beneath a rolling bank of grey-black storm clouds. Grayson threw her a significant glance as they made for the path and scrambled down it, the wind snatching at their clothes and whipping Maggie's hair around her face and neck.

When they got to the car, Grayson handed her the blanket, two smallish boxes and a duffle. 'You okay to carry these up?' At her nod, he said, 'I'll bring the jerry can of water after I park the car.'

Taking care to keep her balance in the strengthening wind, she made her way back to the cave and dumped the gear on the floor. Opening the sealed boxes, she found emergency provisions; matches, tea bags, a billy can, pannikins, long-life milk and sugar sachets, muesli bars, and even packs of two-minute noodles. There was also a first aid kit, a tarpaulin and folded camp shovel, a snake bite kit, and bottles of drinking water.

She took out one of the bottles and hugged it to her breast.

Thank you, Main Roads!

Now for a fire....

She moved the gear nearer the fireplace, where the last human occupants had kindly left a stack of firewood and kindling. She used some paper wrapping to get a blaze going and soon had a comforting glow to see and work by. With the fire crackling away in the corner, she laid out the other boxes of provisions, and the room began to take on a homely feel.

She kept glancing at the tarpaulin and blanket folded against the wall.

One blanket … between the two of us.

A shadow fell as Grayson appeared at the entrance. 'It's starting to come down out there.' Brushing rain off his neck and arms he came inside, dumping a full jerry can near the wall. 'Hey, you've made it cosy in here. Don't need this anymore.' He retrieved the torch, switched it off and pocketed it, before coming to squat beside her.

'Did you find somewhere sheltered for the car?'

'There's another ridge just around from this one, in the lee of the hill. It's not as high so I was able to get the car up onto it using the lowest gear – lucky it's a four wheel drive. I think it'll be elevated enough to stay above any rising water, and should be reasonably sheltered from the wind.'

'You've done well, Gray, for someone who's never experienced a cyclone before.'

He threw her a reproachful grin. '*We've* done the best we can. And what is a cyclone anyway, but a bad storm. I've experienced plenty of them in my time.'

His last words were swallowed up by the loud moaning of the wind and the pelt of heavy rain against the boulders outside. Moving nearer the cave entrance, he peered out at the tempest. 'I hope Billy and Rosie were right about this place, 'cos we're here for the duration now.'

'Well then, I guess we should make ourselves comfortable. Would you like a cup of tea?'

'Great idea. Pass me the billy and I'll fill it from the jerry can.'

. . .

Their hands wrapped around pannikins of hot, sweet tea, they sat with their backs against the rock wall and listened to the storm's growing ferocity. If they leaned to the side, they could see through a gap in the boulders the squalls of horizontal, driving rain carrying with it leaves and twigs and other debris. The wind's howling moan had become a roar as it passed the entrance, every now and then forcing a damp mist to drift all the way to the back of the cave. The second time that happened they donned the wet weather gear they'd found in the duffle.

'Gotta give it to the department,' Grayson said after also finding a battery operated radio/CD player, 'they certainly look after their people.' He tried the radio and wasn't surprised when there was no reception. Muttering, 'Would've been good to stay updated on the cyclone,' he added, 'glad I thought to grab some CDs from the car.' He loaded one, ramping up the volume to drown out the raging wind.

A premature, ominous gloom had fallen outside, while in the cave the firelight flickered around the walls. Combined with the strains of music and the fresh, earthy scent of wet ground, it made a surprisingly pleasant atmosphere.

When he heard the words of the next song, ... *it's been a perfect day, now I hope you'll stay the night ...,* Grayson said drily, 'Like we have a choice,' and they grinned. But when the following lyrics took an increasingly romantic turn, their grins evaporated and they looked away ... anywhere but at each other.

Can't just sit here squirming like a, like a ... ridiculous person.

Maggie got to her feet and put the billy on to boil again. 'Like something to eat, Gray?'

'Why not.' He watched as she opened two noodle packets and set them aside. As soon as the water was boiling, she shook the contents of the packets into it and then sat on her haunches to wait the prescribed two minutes. When she caught Grayson studying her, she hastily looked down at her watch.

Who would've thought two minutes could pass so slowly.

The noodles done, she took the billy off the flame and set it on the sand between them.

'This is it for the crockery and cutlery, I'm afraid.' She handed him a metal camping fork, adding with her nose in the air and a plum in her mouth, 'Jeeves has sent the good silver out for polishing.'

They laughed together and took turns dipping into the billy and loading their forks with the steaming, savoury noodles.

He swallowed a mouthful and nodded his approval. 'Not bad. Just like Mum used to make.'

She gave a shy smile. 'Why thank you, sir. Unfortunately this is a secret recipe, handed down through generations of Perkins, so I can't share it with you. Well, actually I could, but then I'd have to kill you.'

He gave a bark of laughter and loaded his fork again.

'Oh alright, you've twisted my arm.' Maintaining the snooty air, she said in a low, secretive voice, 'It's all in the flavouring, you see. One must know how much is enough. One sachet per serve is just right, but too much is ... well ... too much. And don't get me started on how not enough is simply not enough.' She stuck out her chest and tried to swallow a grin. 'And therein lies the secret of Maggie's world famous two minute noodles.'

He laughed again and she joined in.

To anyone standing outside in the wind and driving rain, being pelted by debris and in danger from ominously creaking overhead tree branches, the sounds of laughter would have seemed bizarre. Inside the cave, the world of its latest 'squatters' had shrunk to a fire-lit cavern on a slope in the back of beyond, and the two people sharing it....

After they'd finished eating and clearing away, Grayson spread the tarpaulin on the ground and they stretched out on it, leaning on their elbows to listen to the music while taking care to stay a 'safe' distance from each other.

A sudden crash near the cave's entrance had them jumping to their feet.

Grayson indicated for Maggie to stay where she was and went to the entrance to peer out. 'Just a tree limb down, I think,' he shouted over the roaring wind, 'quite close by.'

Breathing a sigh of relief, Maggie went to settle on the tarp again when her eye caught nearby movement ... *very* nearby. She was about to say something when Grayson threw a piece of wood on the fire and the bright shower of sparks lit up the area.

And revealed the hairy, hand-sized Wolf spider clinging to her shoulder.

It was edging toward her face, two of its eight legs waving in the air near her cheek, as though searching for another foothold.

She let out a shriek and threw herself against the wall, arms flailing in the air.

Grayson was at her side in an instant. 'What? *What?*'

Her only answer was another shriek, even higher pitched than the first, making him wince. Her wild-eyed thrashing made it impossible for him to see what was wrong, so he grabbed her by an arm. That's when he saw the spider trying desperately to maintain its hold on her shoulder. The more she thrashed, the tighter the arachnid clung.

'Oh,' he chuckled, 'it's just a spider!' and released her arm.

'GET ... IT ... OFF ... ME!' She flapped her hands in the air and danced a knees-up jig on the spot.

He threw back his head and laughed.

'GRAYSON!'

Still laughing, he flicked the unwitting creature off her shirt with a finger. When it hit the floor he squished it under his work boot.

She shuddered and leaped away to stand doubled over, catching her breath. When she could speak again, she puffed, 'Where did *it* come from?'

'Must've been in the wood pile, and crawled out when you disturbed it.' Making spider-like movements with his hand on the cave wall, he announced melodramatically, like a movie trailer voice-over, 'Stealthily scaling the wall behind its unsuspecting prey, the deadly arachnid prepared to launch a lethal attack—'

'Very funny.'

At the sight of her sour expression he dissolved into laughter again.

'Anyway, you didn't have to kill it. I only wanted it off me.'

He grinned, unabashed. 'For all I know it might've been poisonous. And there was every likelihood it would have returned, to maybe crawl over you while you were asleep. I'm sure you wouldn't want that.'

She gave another shudder. 'I take back what I said. I'm *glad* you killed it. Thank you, thank you, thank you.' When she noticed him still trying to bite back laughter, she threw him a disgusted look, which only amused him further.

'You should've seen yourself.' Mirth twinkled in his eyes. 'That was some dance. You should go on that show ... what's it called? Oh yes, *Australia's Got Talent*. Of course you'll need a new dance partner, 'cos I think *his* dancing days are over.' He indicated the splatter mark on the sand with barely suppressed amusement.

She glared at him, arms crossed over her chest. 'I'm *so* pleased you find my terror amusing.'

'Amusing? Hilarious more like it!' He laughed out loud and then wiped his eyes.

'Grayson.'

He tried to suppress another guffaw but failed.

'*Grayson.*'

With another attempt at sobriety that was only marginally successful, he spluttered, 'Yes, Maggie?'

'Do us both a favour and get over it. Oh, and it goes without saying that we will never speak of this again.' That only earned her another bark of laughter. Shoving hands on hips, she said tartly, 'Can you do something *useful* and check if any of his buddies are in here with us, please? I'm sure you don't want to be woken by terrified shrieks during the night.'

He raised his hands in surrender. 'That I don't! One shriek was bad enough.'

When his eyes crinkled at the corners and he gave another splutter, she snapped, 'Look, I think I'll go and sit it out in the car. At least it'll be critter and jester free.' When she moved toward the entrance, he immediately sobered.

'You can't go out there, Maggie, it's not safe.' At her mutinous expression, he once more raised his hands in surrender. 'Okay, okay, I'm checking for any other unwelcome residents.' Taking out his torch again he switched it on and began examining the nooks and crannies in the cave's walls and floor.

Although a big man, his movements were smooth and fluid. When he reached up to steady himself in a narrow corner she could see the firm muscles in his arms flexing, and she recalled how good his hug had felt the other night. Giving herself a mental shake, she dragged her eyes away, sat on the tarp again, and made herself think of Troy.

Troy, who hadn't returned her calls.

She'd tried to reach him numerous times before they left Burketown, without success. While she'd received concerned messages from her workmates and Evie, from her husband there was only silence. Tears pricked her eyes and she squeezed them shut, as one thought pushed itself to the forefront of her mind.

Doesn't my husband care that I might be in danger?

13

Grayson switched off the torch and folded his long frame to sit beside her. 'Well, I'm happy to report no further evidence of arachnid activity. My inspection only turned up some boring old dinosaur bones, prehistoric fossils, and priceless aboriginal artwork.'

Maggie didn't return his grin. Twisting her face away, she said in a choked voice, 'Oh ... g-good.'

He frowned. 'Is everything okay?'

'Yes, of course.'

'It's just that you seem upset. Are you scared?'

'No ... well ... a bit, I guess.'

'We should be safe here. And I don't think you'll be bothered by any more hairy hitchhikers.'

She flicked him a grateful, watery glance. Her eyes appeared huge in the pale oval of her face.

His frown deepened. 'We're going to be here for a while. Is there something you want to talk about?'

So much compassion in that deep voice....

She gazed down at her hands as the words tumbled from her mouth. 'It's nothing, just ... Troy ... hasn't tried to c-contact me this whole time.'

'Oh.'

'Yes, oh.' She sniffed and said in a rush, 'Gray, if your wife was away from home and you heard she might be in danger, wouldn't you be desperate to reach her?'

'Well, sure. But there are lots of reasons why Troy might not be able—'

'Wouldn't you *need* to know sh-she was safe?'

He exhaled. 'I would, yes.'

She threw a hand in the air. 'But then you probably *loved* your wife—' she sucked in a breath, coloured, and snapped her mouth shut.

They sat in silence, not looking at each other. Scooping up a handful of sand from the ground beside him, Grayson slowly opened his fist and watched the sand drain out, saying quietly, 'You don't think Troy loves you?'

'I *know* he doesn't.' She sniffed and wiped the back of a hand across her eyes. 'And *I* don't love *him*. Though goodness knows I've tried.'

Grayson glanced at her. 'Are you saying you don't love him ... any more?'

'I'm saying I've *never* loved him.' She gave a shuddering sigh.

'So....' It was dangerous, he shouldn't ask ... but the words were out before he could stop them. 'So why did you marry him?'

'Well, isn't *that* the million d-dollar qu-question.' Her voice broke, and to her horror a fat tear slid down her cheek.

He hastily looked away, dragging a rough hand through his hair. Acting on impulse, even with the best of intentions, only put him – both of them – on shaky ground. If he was going to comfort her, it would be with words, not actions.

He leaned against the wall and rested an arm on a bent knee. 'You know, marriage is a funny thing. Some people go into it with their eyes open, others with them closed. Some drift into it while others rush headlong in the heat of the moment. Most go in expecting it to last forever, and for some of them, it does. Not all.' A pensive note crept into his voice as though he were thinking aloud. 'There are no guarantees, no "one size fits all", no roadmaps to wedded bliss.' Looking down, he traced a T in the sand beside him with a finger. 'We all simply blunder along as best we can, finding our own way through the marital maze.'

When Maggie turned to face him, he regarded her levelly. 'None of us is perfect. We all make mistakes. Look at me and Tina....'

As he recounted the details of his own failed marriage, she noticed his expression lifting.

'... and so I ended up here, in Australia, on my own.' He raised his chin and with a decisive sweep of a hand, scrubbed out the T he'd written in the sand.

She nodded her understanding while gazing into his face. The public mask was gone. He looked ... liberated.

'I don't know why I told you all that.' He gave a self-conscious huff. 'I was trying to make *you* feel better, but ended up telling you *my* life story – or should that be my *wife* story?'

'Thanks for sharing with me.'

'Lucky you,' he said drily, 'the first person I've burdened with all the gory details.'

'Well, you *have* made me feel a bit better, knowing I'm not the only messed-up person here.'

At her teasing smile he gave an amused grunt.

She went on cautiously. 'And it looks like talking about it did you some good too?'

'I guess....'

'Maybe you just needed to get it off your chest.'

'You're probably right, I just *couldn't* talk about it ... 'til now. Didn't want to have to deal with it, I 'spose.' His lips tipped into a rueful half smile. 'I feel like a coward for avoiding it for so long.'

She spluttered, '*Coward?* Gray, no one in their right mind could ever consider *you* a coward.'

'A shrinking violet then?' His eyes crinkled at the corners.

She chuckled. 'Not even that. Just a human, with imperfections like the rest of us.'

'Thanks.' Nodding slowly, he straightened. 'You know what I miss the most out here?'

'What?'

'A pub. I think after all that soul-searching we could both use a stiff drink. But there's never a pub around when you most need one.'

'Oh yes! A drink would be great right now. I'm feeling ashamed about getting...,' and she pulled a face '... you know ... emotional.'

'C'mon, like you said, we're only human. And this isn't exactly a picnic in the park, is it?' He nudged her with an elbow. 'Don't worry, I live by the creed that what happens in the cave, stays in the cave.'

'And that applies to the spider incident too?'

Puffing out his chest, he stuck his nose in the air and announced in a tone worthy of a high court magistrate, 'I regret to inform you, Madam, that the rule in question does not apply in extreme cases such as that.'

'Oh!'

When she made to swat him on the arm he ducked away, laughing. 'Oh alright, I'll consider it a blanket rule. And speaking of blankets, you take it, I won't need it.' He handed her the folded rug. 'And I 'spose we should try to get some sleep.'

Gratitude shone from her eyes as she took the proffered blanket and settled herself on the tarp, murmuring, 'Goodnight Gray, and ... thanks.'

'Goodnight Maggie.' He watched her curl onto her side and listened as her breathing slowed to a steady rhythm. When the blanket slipped down he leaned over to pull it carefully up to her shoulders again and then stayed there, gazing into her sleeping face. When, with a regretful sigh, he rolled over to lie with his back to her, he listened to the storm's savagery outside but his thoughts were far away....

Waking to find himself under the blanket, he lifted his head to see only a body-shaped indentation in the tarp beside him. A quick scan of the cave revealed Maggie sitting at the entrance, chin resting on arms crossed over her knees. She was framed in a shaft of early morning sunlight, which made her skin shine a satiny honey-gold and her hair shimmer as though touched with a gilded brush.

Clasping his hands behind his head he gazed at her, savouring both the appealing image and his new-found sense of freedom, the feeling he'd been released from emotional bondage.

As though aware of his scrutiny she turned from surveying the tranquil, albeit decimated, countryside, and smiled. 'Morning sleepyhead.'

He yawned and stretched. 'Morning.'

'Well, it looks to me like you need a caffeine injection to get moving.' She rose to her feet, dusting the sand from her pants and heading to the fireplace to rake the embers.

He grinned and lifted himself onto his elbows, running a hand over his head and darkly stubbled chin. 'Did you sleep alright?'

'Yeah, surprisingly.'

'Sounds like the storm's gone.'

'Yep, the "fun" is all over.'

'Do you know if we still have a car?'

She stopped what she was doing to glance at him. 'I hadn't got around to checking.'

'How long have you been up?'

'Only long enough to chase away an unwanted visitor.' She grinned at his blank look. 'Just a brown snake with ideas of joining us in here.'

'What? A *snake?*' He frowned and then scoffed, 'Oh yeah, *sure,*' until he noticed her expression. 'You *are* kidding?'

'Go see for yourself. I think it's still out there, a little way past the rocks in front of the entrance. I was watching to make sure it didn't do an illegal U-turn and come back in.'

'You chased a snake? No way!' Leaping to his feet he went to the entrance and looked out, in time to see a sinewy brown tail slither down the stony slope and disappear into the scrub. He returned, shaking his head in disbelief. 'I'm impressed ... gobsmacked, actually. You freak out about a spider and then, without a scream – or any sound at all – you calmly dispatch a poisonous snake?'

'I had the shovel handy in case it needed persuading. And unlike the spider, the snake wasn't actually *on* me. That makes all the difference.' A grin tugged at the corners of her lips.

He gave a bark of laughter. 'Maggie Perkins, you are a marvel.'

After a makeshift breakfast of muesli bars and instant coffee, Maggie re-packed the gear while Grayson went to check on the car. As he clambered over fallen tree limbs, waded through piles of leaf litter and sodden vegetation and jumped puddles between rocks, his apprehension grew.

Rounding the embankment, he spotted a gleam of white amid the storm debris, and swore under his breath. Feet slipping on the wet surfaces, he made for the fleet vehicle and found it covered in layers of leaves, twigs, and even muddy gravel.

And then he saw a tree branch protruding from the smashed back window like a timber javelin and swore again, loudly.

He felt his way around the car, checking the full extent of the damage, and found the side closest to the slope virtually untouched. The body panels on the exposed side had taken a beating but thankfully all four wheels appeared okay.

He opened a door, gingerly, and scanned the interior. Apart from rainwater pooling on the floor beneath the broken window and a damp back seat, it appeared otherwise undamaged. He exhaled through pursed lips and turned his attention to the offending branch.

It would have to come out before they could go anywhere.

Maggie stacked the last box at the base of the path and straightened to wipe the sweat from under her eyes and nose. In the wake of the cyclone the outside air was still, oppressive, and hotter than in the cave. She glanced around. No sign of Grayson. It was taking him a while to check on the car....

'Gray?'

No answer.

Making her way through the drenched scrub, she stopped when she spotted him near the debris-covered vehicle.

'O-oh.' As she hurried to join him she surveyed the surrounding trees. 'Where'd that big branch come from? There's not a tree that size within cooee. Must've been carried here by the wind.'

Grayson was tugging at the stubborn limb, testing if it were firmly embedded. Sweat glistened on his skin, and his cotton shirt clung damply to his body.

'Hang on Gray, let me help you.' She moved closer to peer through the window. 'Those twigs at the end of the branch might be anchoring it.' She clambered around the car, slipping in the slimy leaf litter and steadying herself against the vehicle.

Grayson wiped his face with an equally sweaty forearm and rested on his haunches. 'So much for finding a sheltered parking spot.'

When she reached the end of the branch she snapped off the first of the offending twigs and glanced across at him. 'There's no way you could've done better. The car's still drive-able isn't it?'

'I think so.'

'Well then, you did great.'

'I hope the fleet guys see it that way.'

'They will.' She broke off some more twigs while Grayson rose to wrestle the branch from side to side to loosen its hold. 'Look, we all know what cyclones are like. First they blow from one direction, then they turn and attack from the opposite direction. And this one hit the mainland as a category *five* ... that's some force. There's no way you could've kept the car from being damaged. You did brilliantly just keeping it from being totally wrecked.'

'Thanks.' he positioned himself squarely at the back of the car. 'Okay, let's give this another go.' Shoving his sleeves up to his elbows, he braced himself with legs wide apart, work pants stretched tightly over his straining physique. His arm muscles bulged as he gripped the recalcitrant branch and threw his weight back with a grunt, heaving the branch with him. After a brief instant of resistance, the limb came away with a tearing, shattering sound, leaving in its wake a jagged hole dripping glass fragments.

Grayson manhandled the branch to the edge of the ridge and pushed it over, out of the way. Dusting his hands, he looked across at Maggie. 'You might want to call home base on the two-way, and—' He stopped when he noticed her wince and touch tentative fingers to her cheek. 'What happened?'

'One of the twigs bent back and then flicked across my face.' She lowered her hand and stared at the blood on her fingertips as he hurried to her side, swearing under his breath.

'I thought you'd removed all the twigs, otherwise I would've waited—'

'I couldn't break this one, it was too tough.' Seeing his expression she hastened to add, 'It's not your fault, Gray. I should've moved out of the way.'

'Here, let me see the damage.' Taking her face in his

hands, he wiped away the blood with a thumb and peered at the already swelling spot where the rough twig had sliced into her skin. His brow furrowed. 'Lucky it missed your eye. Where's the first aid kit?'

With his strong, workmanlike hands gently cupping her face, his manly scent in her nose, and their bodies so close, she could feel raw energy arcing between them. Her voice was reedy when she answered, 'In the gear, at the base of the path. But don't worry, it's only a scratch. No big deal.'

She made herself focus on his thickening five o'clock shadow and then watched a drop of sweat trace a damp path from his temple down the side of his mud-smudged face. When her eyes alighted on his firm mouth, she took a quick breath and looked away.

'It needs a dressing. With your soft skin, it could be quite a deep cut.' He lowered his hands and made to move away ... until their eyes met, and locked.

The undercurrent of desire she'd been fighting to keep in check surged, flooding Maggie's every cell. She couldn't move or look away, just stood gazing at him, face tipped upward and her body leaning toward his of its own accord.

Grayson's eyes flicked down to her mouth and he felt the lure, like the relentless drag of the tide. And when her full, trembling lips parted as though in supplication, he sucked in a ragged breath. When he raised his eyes to meet hers, he found himself gazing into dark, sensual pools.

He could feel himself free-falling into them....

She's married, his inner voice cautioned blurrily.

But it's a loveless marriage, she told me so herself. So does it still count?

No.

Gripping her arms gently, he bent his head until his lips hovered just above hers. She continued gazing into his eyes as though drowning in them.

Did it count with Tina?

Damn!

He stiffened, and when a tiny whimper escaped Maggie's throat – the strongest protest she could muster at that point – it was enough to make him let her go and step back. She blinked, swaying on the spot, while he stood a few feet away, silent but for the sound of his own harsh breathing.

Maggie finally broke the charged silence. Taking a deep breath, she cleared her throat and said in what she hoped was a conversational tone, 'Think I'll ... um ... radio home base and let them know we're okay.'

His eyes raked over her face and settled on the darkening crimson welt. He frowned and said thickly, 'First get a dressing for that. There should be plasters and ointment in the first aid kit.'

She hurried away, heart still hammering in her chest.

It was *her* fault that happened. *She* had turned an innocent moment into a passionate one. *She* had changed things between them just as they'd found a firm footing.

She gave a dry sob.

She had allowed her heart to overrule her head.

Angry, guilt-ridden tears stung her eyes as she dug the first aid kit out of the gear and extracted an alcohol swab, tube of antiseptic cream, and a packet of plasters. Then she paused to rest on her haunches, head down, taking deep breaths to slow her heart rate and settle her nerves.

When she felt stronger, she made her way back to the car, where Grayson was clearing away more storm debris from around it. Climbing into the passenger side, she turned the rear-view mirror so she could see her face and wiped away a coagulating dribble of blood. It was a nasty scratch but not too deep. The alcohol-soaked swab stung and left her gasping and flapping a hand while waiting for it to dry. Once sure the wound was clean, she applied the ointment and then stuck a plaster over it.

Done.

Switching on the two way radio, she was relieved when it crackled into life. There was no doubting the relief in Harry's voice too, when she called up home base and he came on.

She hastened to assure him they were okay and then cut to the chase. 'Harry, the car's suffered some damage, but Grayson thinks it's still driveable, over.' She glanced out to see Grayson donning a pair of rigger's gloves from the car's toolkit. When he began removing the broken glass from the smashed window, she lowered her voice. 'He feels bad about the car, Harry, but he did a great job in the circumstances. Over.'

'As long as it gets you both home safely, I don't care about the car. Over.'

Maggie gave a small smile. It was so like her boss to value people over assets. She signed off, promising to give him an update once they were on their way.

. . .

Once he'd freed it from the worst of the debris, Grayson started the car and listened to the motor for a few seconds. Putting it in gear he eased off the embankment and then inched around the ridge to park as close as he could to the stack of gear, where Maggie stood waiting. They spoke barely a word as they loaded the car. Their fleeting camaraderie had been blown away, as if by the cyclone's gale-force winds.

And who's fault is that?

Her lips tightened.

'That's everything, I think.' He wiped his hands on his pants without looking at her.

She gazed into the distance. 'Yep.'

'Right then, let's go.'

They climbed in, but Grayson didn't immediately start the car. He sat without speaking, hands gripping and un-gripping the steering wheel. Beside him Maggie kept her eyes downcast, trying not to dwell on what had almost happened between them and how intensely she had longed for it *to* happen. When she heard him finally turn the key in the ignition, she glanced across to see him staring through the windscreen at the storm-ravaged landscape, his grip now firm on the wheel.

With an audible sigh, he put the car into gear and said in a low, gravelly voice, 'Well, if I had to weather a tropical cyclone, I'm glad it was with you, marvellous Maggie.'

All she could do was stare at him, wide-eyed and mute, as they headed toward the highway and home.

14

'Well, you've had a few days to recover from your rather eventful trip to the gulf. Everything back to normal now?' Harry indicated a tub chair in front of his desk.

Maggie nodded as she took a seat, smiling at the fatherly concern in his eyes.

'And how's that going?' He pointed at her cheek.

She touched the scab with a finger. 'Pretty much healed. Should only leave a tiny scar, if anything.'

'A memoir of the trip, hey?'

'Mm.'

'And thankfully the only injury.'

Not quite.

Her face clouded.

My integrity took a beating too.

Harry was running his eyes over the paperwork in front

of him. 'Right, better get down to it. We've got a few things to go over this morning.'

As he listed the items for discussion, Maggie moved her chair closer to the desk. She needed to wrap herself in her professional persona again and stop fretting about whatever this *thing* was with Grayson. It was foolish to get so wound-up about what was surely just an infatuation, a ridiculous school-girl crush with the added lure of the forbidden.

Or was this the real deal? Was Grayson the man she'd been waiting for ... *should* have waited for ... but didn't?

Her stomach clenched.

'Are you sure you feel alright?' Harry leaned forward to scrutinise her face.

She swallowed. 'I'm fine.'

'You seem distracted. And you're very pale.'

'Guess I'm just ... a bit tired.' She attempted a smile.

'If you need some time off just go ahead and take it. You know that, right?'

'I will, don't worry. Now, you were saying we should develop a procedure to handle situations like Gray ... ahem ... Grayson and I encountered?' Her lips tightened.

Mustn't let my voice catch whenever I say his name, and mustn't say it too often, even if my tongue longs to feel it and my ears, to hear it.

Harry was nodding. 'It could easily happen again, and not everyone is as sensible as you two.'

Sensible?

She gave a silent humph.

Not lately....

'Natural disasters can strike at any time,' Harry was saying, 'and we need to be prepared. There's another big cyclone season predicted for next year....'

'Good, that's done. Now, there's one last item not on the list. It's Reeves. I want to offer him a permanent position here.'

She sucked in a breath.

Grayson, living here in Cloncurry.

Working just down the corridor from her office.

Bumping into her in the lunch room, the Stubby Hut, at every work and social function.

She blinked hard and found Harry staring at her.

He expected a response, a *sensible* response, but all she could think of was *stall!*

'Oh ... um ... I see. But ... um ... we don't currently have a vacant professional officer position, Harry. They're all filled by permanent or long-term relieving staff.'

'We *didn't* have a position, but we do now.' He puffed out his chest. 'I managed to secure one from the departmental pool, through my connections with the Establishment Unit.'

'Oh?' Her voice shook. She took a hasty swallow.

'He's worth it, Maggie.' Harry leaned back and threaded his fingers together beneath his chin. 'I've had good reports from everyone he's had dealings with, professionals and the public alike. I was also impressed with his handling of the situation in the gulf. And the blokes in the engineering group respect the hell out of him, so he'd be a great mentor for the more junior engineers. I can see only benefits to having him here with us on a permanent basis ... if we can jag it.'

'Oh.'

Is that all I can say, 'Oh'? Am I reduced to a one-word vocabulary now?

Harry frowned. 'You don't have any reservations, surely, after your glowing account of his performance under stress? If you do, I need to hear them now.'

'No!' She gave a vigorous head shake. 'No reservations at all ... about his suitability. Grayson is an asset to the department, no doubt about it.'

'But?'

'But....'

If he stays here, that'll be the end of my marriage, nothing surer. And part of me still wants to hang on, work things out with Troy, do Mum and Dad proud.

Her brain finally snapped to attention.

'He's on a four-five-seven visa, Harry. So until he applies for, and is granted, permanent Australian residency, we could only ever regard Grayson as temporary. At any time he could decide to return to the UK. And he'd need to receive his Certified Practising Engineer accreditation from Engineers Australia before we could offer him a *real* permanent appointment.'

Harry gave a pleased murmur. 'Yes, but I have plans on that score as well.'

Her heart sank. 'Oh?'

There's that word again.

'We'll sponsor his residency application and support his

CPE accreditation bid, that'll make the deal all the more appealing. Assuming he's successful in obtaining both – and I have no reason to think he won't be – we'll get to keep him here, at least for a while.' Looking up from his paperwork, Harry said with crisp authority, 'Go ahead and make him the offer, Maggie.'

She opened her mouth ... and then closed it again. His tone elicited no further discussion, so what more could she do but nod and leave? Her limbs felt heavy, sluggish, as she rose and made her way to her office, where she slumped in the chair and stared blindly at her computer's screensaver. When her phone shrilled, she jumped and snatched up the receiver.

'I forgot to mention that I want this to be a promotion for Reeves, so make it a level five. I'm sure you can come up with a role description if we don't already have one.'

She closed her eyes and exhaled. 'Yes, Harry.'

'And I want to move on this quickly, so could you catch Grayson before he and Tom head to the Sweet Creek site this morning? We need to fill that position ASAP or we'll lose it.' Harry's tone grew smug. 'And I want to give Reeves time to realise what a great opportunity this is.'

'Sure, Harry. I'll see if I can catch him now.' After slowly replacing the receiver, she sat staring at it and then sighed and pushed herself to her feet.

Better get this over and done with.

As she strode along the corridor she could feel her heart drumming in her chest, and her tongue sticking to the roof of her mouth.

I shouldn't feel like this. I'm on my way to offer someone a job, something I've done a hundred times before. This is no different.

But it was, and she knew it.

As she approached the door to Grayson's office she prayed he'd be out so she could just leave a note asking him to see Harry, who was so pleased with himself he'd probably be glad to be the bearer of good news. And save her from having to do it.

When she poked her head around the doorway and saw Grayson at his desk, punching figures into the computer, her heart soared while her courage plummeted. He glanced up, stiffened, and then gestured for her to enter.

Gathering her courage, she strode in and said matter-of-factly, 'Got a minute, Gray...son?'

'Sure, Maggie. Have a seat.'

Her treacherous heart gave a wiggle at the richness of his deep voice.

I *will* project calm professionalism if it *kills* me.

Easing herself into the chair and taking care to maintain a non-committal expression, she steeled herself to meet his eyes. Their deep, slate-grey colour reminded her of the sky on a sleety morning.

With the faint glow of a cave fire in their depths....

She gave herself a mental shake and said more sharply than intended, 'Harry asked me to come and see you.'

'Oh yes?'

'He wants me to make you an offer.'

'What sort of offer?'

She bristled.

I'm in HR, what else would I be offering but a job?

'A promotion, Grayson, to level five. And a permanent position here in Cloncurry office.' When all he did was gaze at her, she hurried on. 'I'll get a role description to you as soon as I can, so you know what you'd be agreeing to.'

There, I've said it.

As if sensing she was about to leave, he leaned forward to rest both arms on the desk. 'Why?'

She frowned, perplexed. 'What?'

'Why is Harry offering me this job?'

'Because he thinks you'll be a valuable addition to our engineering team.'

'Is that the only reason?'

In the face of his unblinking gaze she lowered her eyes to stare at her hands. 'Well ... he ... um ... Harry, that is ... said he's had nothing but good reports about you. And the guys respect you.' She took a breath. 'He believes you'll increase our pool of engineering expertise, and be a good mentor for our junior engineers.'

That's it, stick to business.

'I see. And what do *you* think about the offer?'

She looked up to gauge his expression and found herself whisked back to Black Mountain, feeling again the anticipation, longing, *ache* for his kiss....

'Maggie?'

She swallowed and gave her head an imperceptible shake. 'Sorry ... um ... what was the question?'

'I was asking what you think about this job offer.'

She took another calming breath. 'I think it's a great opportunity for you to fast-track your career.'

'No, I want to know what it means for *you.*'

Stay professional.

She gave a half-hearted chuckle. 'It means more work for me, as do all Harry's requests. He doesn't realise how much paperwork is involved in making his plans a reality....' Her voice trailed off as Grayson stared at her, tight-lipped.

Leave.

Now.

She got to her feet, just as he said quietly, 'I'd like to talk about this some more but Tom and I have to go out shortly, and we won't be back 'til late.'

'Oh.' Her forehead creased. 'Harry wants to move on this quickly.'

'Well ... maybe I could meet you for a drink after work?'

Her whole being swelled with longing.

Meeting after hours? Not a good idea.

Come on, it's only a drink in a public place.

Don't do it!

But Harry wants this sorted, and soon....

Realising Grayson was waiting for a response, she said rashly, 'Alright. What say we meet at the PO around six?'

At his nod she turned and walked out, feeling his eyes on her every step of the way.

Grayson was focused on negotiating the rough gravel track to Sweet Creek when beside him Tom said, 'I wonder if we're about to lose our Maggie. Did she say anything to you, Reevers?'

He stiffened. 'Why would she tell *me* anything personal?'

Tom's eyes narrowed. 'Well, I'm assuming the two of you got quite close while you were away. Sheltering in a cave overnight and all that.'

Grayson ignored the dig. 'Am I supposed to guess what you're talking about, or are you going to tell me?'

'Just wondering if what I've heard is true. Y'never know with second or third-hand news.' Tom turned his gaze to the road ahead. 'The word around town is that Troy Kerr's been offered a job in Western Australia, with BHP Mining.'

Grayson's ears pricked and he couldn't resist a sideways glance at Tom, who was watching him with shrewd eyes. He gave a nonchalant shrug. 'News to me.'

Tom raised an eyebrow. 'Apparently Troy-boy's openly spruiking that he's accepted the job, but is tight-lipped about Maggie's feelings on the subject.' He gave a cynical snort. 'Maybe he hasn't told *her* yet. And that's not the worst of it. Word has it that when someone asked him outright what his wife thinks of the move, he said she can tag along if she wants, or not. Reckons either's fine by him. Can you *believe* that guy?'

The car shuddered as Grayson's foot slipped off the accelerator. When Tom flicked him a questioning glance, he shrugged and powered on again.

15

After walking home from the office, Maggie was taking out her keys to unlock the front door when it opened from inside. A smiling Troy leaned out to give her a peck on the cheek.

'Hey, babe. How was your day?' Without waiting for an answer, he turned and headed back upstairs.

What was with the loving greeting?

She stared after him.

Perhaps something *had* sunk in from yesterday.

She'd been stewing for days, so when he came home from his latest extended work shift it was to a *very* chilly reception.

He had stomped inside in his steel-capped boots, high-vis workwear smelling strongly of metal and motor oil, and stopped when he saw her glaring at him from the kitchen. 'Oh, you're home,' he said cautiously. 'When did you get back?'

'A few days ago.' She thrust both hands on her hips. 'Not that you care.'

He stared at her blankly.

'You have no idea, do you?' She shook her head at him. 'I felt abandoned out there, Troy, by the *one* person who should've been *desperate* to know I was safe. Other people got in touch to check I was okay, but there was nothing from you.' When he didn't speak, she charged on.

'I don't understand how you could've ignored my phone messages, I left enough of them. Or how you could be so blasé, considering where I was and what was happening there. You *do* realise that cyclones are life-threatening? That I could've been injured or killed?'

She refrained from mentioning anything about Grayson's involvement. He was best left out of the discussion for a whole host of reasons.

'I was preoccupied with work.' As he spoke, Troy's lips tightened into a mulish line.

How she hated that look. If she were Evie, she'd slap it off his face. Luckily for him she wasn't Evie.

'And anyway, it's the department's responsibility to make sure you're safe when they send you away on business.' When that only earned him an incredulous scowl, he resorted to the same strategy he used whenever they disagreed on anything. He walked off, dashing Maggie's hopes of clearing the air between them and maybe – just maybe – bringing them closer.

Knowing further words would just bounce off his hard shell of pig-headedness, she'd spent a disappointed, angry, and frustrated night in the guest room.

With a sigh, she followed him up the stairs. Had a change of heart prompted Troy's unusually warm greeting, or a guilty conscience?

Unlikely. He seemed impervious to both....

She sighed again.

I never used to be so cynical.

After putting away her work bag and kicking off her shoes, she joined him in the kitchen. Perching on the bench, she dangled her feet like a kid just home from school and allowed him to fuss over her.

Why not enjoy it when it happens, which isn't often.

'Wine?' At her nod he poured her a glass and asked again, 'How was your day?'

She began to tell him until she realised he was only half listening.

When her voice trailed off he came to stand directly in front of her. 'Maggie, I want to tell you something.'

She took a sip of wine and eyed him.

'I feel bad about what you said last night. You were right, I was a mongrel for not returning your calls from Bourke ... ville ... er ... town ....' He frowned and clicked his tongue. 'Wherever it was you were.'

She raised a reproving eyebrow but said nothing.

'In my defence, though, you're so damn self-sufficient, it's easy to forget you're just a woman.' Seeing the change in her expression, he hastened to add, 'You know what I mean. You're a woman, obviously,' and he rested a hand on her knee, 'but you usually don't need my help, and I forget that sometimes you might.'

Pursing her lips, she tilted her head and decided to accept that as a compliment, but when he moved closer to take her face in his hands, she had to stop herself from pulling away. Unlike Grayson's, Troy's hands felt rough against her skin and smelled strongly of hand cleaner and oil, and his fingers dug into the tender spot on her cheek. When he bent his head to press his lips against hers, she fought the impulse to twist away.

This is my husband. Kissing him can't feel like a betrayal.

Lifting his head, he gazed into her eyes. 'I love you, babe. You know that, don't you?'

She stared at him. This wasn't like Troy at all.

Hang on ... maybe this was the opportunity she'd been hoping for.

She took a deep breath. 'Troy, can we talk? I mean *really* talk. We don't do that much anymore.'

His hands slipped from her face as he took a step back. 'Sure we do. We're talking now, aren't we?'

'Yes, but—'

'Anyhow talk's cheap, as they say.' He turned to pour himself another drink, his body language all self-satisfaction.

And when he threw an imperious, 'So, what's for dinner?' over his shoulder, Maggie's mouth fell open.

'What's for *dinner*? That's your idea of talking through our problems? Surely you don't think a little lovey-dovey performance can make up for your inconsiderate, callous behaviour?' Seeing the firm set of his mouth, she sprang down from the counter. 'Well excuse me for wanting us to actually *discuss* it.' She stormed off, throwing over her shoulder, 'I have no idea what you're having for dinner, Troy. I'm going out.'

'What? Wait! Maggie...?'

She marched into the bedroom and kicked the door closed behind her. Tearing off her work clothes, she pulled on her favourite jeans and shrugged into a checked shirt. Standing at the mirror to flick a brush through her loose hair, she eyed the angry flush in her cheeks.

Won't need any rouge tonight....

Troy's kiss lingered damply on her mouth, so she went to the bathroom and cleaned her teeth before smoothing gloss on her lips.

Right, I'm ready.

She took a deep breath and returned to the kitchen, where she found Troy leaning against the counter, obviously waiting for her. When she appeared, his sulky expression changed to one of hope. The transition only made her more angry.

Is that how I look to him most of the time, kind of needy and pathetic?

She hardened her heart as he stepped forward and took

her hands in his. 'I thought we could have dinner at home tonight?'

Tugging her hands free, she headed to the door. 'I've got to go out, and I'm not sure how long I'll be.'

When he blurted, 'Maggie, we're moving to Western Australia,' she stopped dead and then spun around to gape at him. He moved closer as his voice took on a wheedling note. 'I've been offered a great job with BHP Mining ... and I've accepted it.'

Her jaw dropped. 'What?'

'They're offering me almost double what I'm making here—'

'But ... Western Australia?'

'Yeah. Great, hey?'

'No, it's *not* great.' Her expression darkened. 'Troy, we've had this discussion before. You know how I feel about giving up my job to move to the other side of the country, so far from everyone and everything I care about.'

'Except me, of course.'

'What?'

'You said you'd be moving away from everyone you care about. Except me.'

'Yes.' She waved a hand in an impatient gesture. 'Yes ... of course.'

'Anyway, you'll come to terms with the move,' he said loftily, 'like you did here. You'll get another job, and make new friends.' He tried to grab her hands again but she moved out of reach.

'It's not only that. Like I've told you before, I'd lose a

truckload of entitlements if I left the Public Service now. I thought you understood that?'

He said nothing, simply crossed his arms and stared at her, his expression mulish.

That *damn* look again.

'Oh, right,' she snapped, 'so it's all decided, is it?'

He shrugged a shoulder.

'You've gone ahead and accepted the job without discussing it with me?'

He scowled. 'I knew you'd turn it into another fight otherwise—'

'So you decided the best strategy was to jump right in, make it a "done deal" so I'd simply have to toe the line?' Anger glinted in her eyes.

'Why can't you be pleased for me? I've been offered a great job for cryin' out loud.'

'Oh sure, I should be *thrilled* you're once again doing what you want without even considering the impact on me, your *wife.*'

His face hardened. 'I think you're forgetting that *I'm* the man in this relationship, Maggie. And the bottom line is, I have the right to decide what's best for us.'

She rolled her eyes. 'Oh *p-lease!* You think your *gender* gives you the right to dictate our ... *my* ... future? That I have no say in it?'

'Say what you like. I've been patient long enough. I'm sick of being stuck out here in the middle of nowhere, just because it suits *you.*'

She gasped and stared wide-eyed at him. 'I can't *believe*

you're blaming me, when it was *your* idea for us to come to Cloncurry! I've simply made the best of it.'

'Go ahead, twist things to suit yourself.'

'Oh!' She gave a bleak laugh and threw up her hands. 'That's rich, coming from you.' She struggled to keep her voice even. 'Here's another "bottom line" for you, Troy. I'm *not* going to Western Australia.'

His lips curled into a snarl. 'Well, Maggie, I *am* going, and you can either tag along or ... make your own arrangements.'

'Tag along—' She stared open-mouthed at him as he shrugged again, sauntered to the nearest lounge chair, and flopped into it. After gazing at the top of his head for a few minutes, she whirled around, yanked open the door and stormed out, leaving him glowering at the blank television screen.

Grayson glanced at his watch. It was long past knock-off time. No wonder the building was pin-drop quiet, he was probably the only person still there. Suppressing a gut tremor at the thought of where he was going and who he was meeting after he left the office, he shut down the computer and got to his feet.

At the door, he turned to flick a final glance around the office and spotted the black mug, the one Tina had given him, standing like a dark, mute sentinel amid the piles of plans, folders and paperwork. He stared at it for a long moment before going to the desk and picking it up. Turning it over in his hands, he recalled the day she had given it to him, all the places he'd taken it, and all that had happened since it came into his life ... and Tina went out of it.

He looked up again, a new resolve in his eyes. Squaring his shoulders, he held the mug over the wastepaper bin ... and released his grip. It slipped from his fingers to land with a sharp *thunk* and a cracking of porcelain. With a satisfied grunt, Grayson turned on his heel and strode from the room, switching off the light as he went and closing the door behind him with a firm click.

When Maggie stepped through the batwing doors of the Post Office Hotel, she saw Grayson leaning against the bar, watching for her.

As she walked over to him, he straightened and dipped his head in greeting, before saying in the dark-chocolate voice she'd grown to love, 'Get you a drink?'

'Yes please, I'll have—'

'A sauv blanc?' At her smiling nod, he lifted his chin to the barman, who reached behind and took a full wine glass out of the floor-to-ceiling bar fridge. 'I ordered you one already, hope that's okay?'

She smiled up at him again, and when he turned to order himself another beer, eyed him from under her lashes, taking in his damp hair, clean polo shirt over well-fitting dark blue jeans, and his trademark work boots. Not wanting to be caught ogling him, she turned to glance around the lounge bar. There were only a few other patrons, all clustered around the drink service area.

Grayson indicated a table in the far corner. 'I thought we might sit over there.' At Maggie's nod, he took the dripping beer stein from the barman and led the way. The lighting in that corner was dim and there was nobody within earshot.

They put their drinks on the table but remained standing, awkward with each other.

Someone put a coin in the jukebox and a popular country song floated across the room.

Goin' the wrong way, down a one way road....

Bending his head, Grayson muttered, 'Hope that's not prophetic.'

'Sorry Gray, did you say something?'

He shook his head and regarded her intently, his eyes creased at the corners as though smiling but his mouth an uncertain line. Raising his glass, he took another drink.

She watched him tip the cold beer down his throat. 'Wow, thirsty hey?'

His only response was to exhale, wipe the back of a hand across his mouth, and put the now empty glass on the table. Bending to lean on his elbows, he kept hold of the stein, staring into the dregs of foam in its base. Maggie eyed him.

He did say he wanted to talk ... didn't he?

As if knowing what she was thinking, he rose to his full height again and fixed her with an intense gaze.

'Maggie, about that job offer....'

'Yes?'

Spying the bartender heading to their table, intent on collecting Grayson's glass and offering him a refill, Grayson gave a forbidding shake of his head. The man propped and then scurried back to the bar.

Grayson turned to Maggie again. 'Before I make a decision, we need to talk about something.'

'Oh?' She squeaked the word.

THAT word. That same *damn* word....

Although a flicker of amusement crossed Grayson's face, his mouth remained a firm line. 'I want to accept the job, but there would be conditions.'

She swallowed, trying to dislodge her heart from her mouth. Her voice came out a little strangled. 'Well, I'm sure Harry would be happy to discuss terms with you—'

'No, Maggie. My conditions don't involve Harry. They involve you.'

She tensed.

Absently rubbing the still-dewy stein with his thumb, he took a breath and went on. 'I'm not sure what the situation is with you and Troy at the moment, but from what I've seen and heard....' He paused as though gathering his thoughts. 'You told me yourself things aren't great between you.' With an audible exhale he ran a large, agitated hand over his hair. 'Look, I need to lay my cards on the table.'

She swallowed.

'I know this may not be the best moment, but my six weeks here are almost up, so I don't have the luxury of time. I need to know where I stand.' He fixed her with a penetrating gaze. 'Maggie, I'll only accept the position if you want me to stay.'

Her eyes widened.

Is he talking to Maggie the woman, or Maggie the HR officer? Not that it matters really, they both want him to stay ... one a whole lot more than the other.

The glass tipped in her hand, spilling wine on the table. She barely noticed.

Grayson ploughed on, his expression determined, his deep voice gritty. 'What I'm asking is ... do we have a future together, you and me?'

She gasped and stared into his eyes. They held an intensity of feeling that took her breath away.

Is this true? Does Grayson feel the same for me as I do for him?

Her heart swelled in her chest, its joyous pounding rising into her throat.

Hang on! Where does that leave me and Troy?

She felt her heart give a shrug.

Troy doesn't love me so what does it matter?

Of course it matters, we're married! Did those vows we took mean nothing? Were they just empty words?

Another heart-shrug.

What would Mum and Dad think if they could see me now?

As the war raged between her mind and heart, Maggie had a sudden image of her mother standing in the kitchen, hands on aproned hips, laughing at the sight of her young daughter hunched over her homework, pouting.

'*Prune* sandwiches, Mum! They're even worse than the brown sugar on brown bread ones.'

Gwen chuckled at her sulky expression. 'I make them

'specially for you, Maggie love. Don't you like having *special* lunches that nobody else has?'

'Yes, but—'

'And prunes are *very* good for you.'

'But they taste funny. And everyone laughs at my lunches, they think they're silly.'

'Maggie.' Coming close to take her daughter's small hands in her floury ones, Gwen said gently, 'First of all, love, not everything good for you will taste or feel good. And secondly, when you're older you'll make up your own mind about things, and not worry what other people think.'

The loving image faded. Maggie pressed her lips together as her mother's words rang in her head.

Grayson was searching her face. 'That's all I need to know to make my decision, Maggie. If your answer is no, just say so. I'll go home to Brisbane when my six weeks are up and won't bother you again. But if your answer is yes, I'll assume I'm right about your marriage being over.' He lifted his chin. 'Despite how this might sound, I'm not the kind of chap who goes around making moves on other men's wives.'

Drawing a deep breath, he gazed into her eyes. 'Let me be clear on this, Maggie. I'm not looking for an affair. That's not an option I would ever consider, no matter how much I want you.'

16

'No matter how much I want you.'

Grayson's words kept replaying in Maggie's head as she walked home from the pub. Although spoken in a voice that felt like a warm caress, their meaning was tearing her apart. The tears she'd been holding in check stung her eyes and she slowed her pace.

Need to compose myself before going home to Troy.

Troy.

What had he been saying around town? Blabbing about the BHP job offer, no doubt, and sparking more gossip about their 'rocky' marriage.

Rocky? That's putting it mildly.

She took a gulp of air and put a quivering hand to her forehead.

Oh hell, I'm a mess! I can't go home like this. Then again, would Troy even notice I'm upset? Probably not. He isn't attuned to my moods, and even if he were, he wouldn't be much bothered by them.

In her head she heard again Grayson's gentle, 'Is everything okay?' when she'd become upset in the cave, and a sob burst from her. She sank to the edge of the footpath, crossed her arms over her knees and buried her face in them, and gave in to the anguish of unquenchable longing, crippling guilt, failure, and loss. Sobs racked her body until she started to hiccup, and raised her head.

I've been down before, when I lost Mum and Dad. I managed to get back up then and I can do it again now.

Taking out a handful of tissues, she wiped her tear-sodden face and blew her nose. Gazing up at the star-filled sky, she let the night air soothe her stinging eyes, before getting to her feet and trudging home.

She let herself in with barely a sound.

The house was quiet, no football commentary blaring from the television, for a change. She checked her watch and frowned. It was still early, surely Troy hadn't gone to bed already? He normally stayed up watching TV until well after she'd fallen asleep. She pushed open the door into the lounge room. The only light came from the TV, where a football match was playing on the screen with the volume turned down to a whisper.

When she flicked on the overhead light, Troy got up from where he'd been sprawled on the couch to stare at her. With a sullen, 'It's about time you got home,' he moved closer, and noticed her red-rimmed eyes. His accusatory tone mellowed to one of concern. 'Hey, what's wrong?'

She opened her mouth but couldn't answer. It felt like her throat had closed over. The only sound she could manage was a choked sob.

'Oh Maggie.' He wrapped his arms around her. 'Don't cry. I forgive you. Everything will be alright, you'll see.'

Taking a deep breath and making herself ignore the 'I forgive you' comment, she let him hold her, closing her eyes and resting her head against his chest. If only she could share her burdens with him ... but that was a vain wish. He hadn't even asked what was wrong, had simply assumed she felt bad about arguing with him earlier.

When she finally mumbled against his shirt, 'Troy, I'm tired. I'm going to bed,' he let her go with what she sensed was relief.

'Okay, babe, you do that. I'll be in when this match is finished.' He put a finger under her chin and tipped her face upward. 'We'll talk in the morning, okay?'

Knowing it was yet another empty promise, meant to deflect any attempts at conversation then and there, she nodded her head numbly and dragged herself along the hallway to the bathroom. She took care to lock the door before stripping and turning on the shower. Stepping under the steaming water, she let it cascade over her head and down her body.

If only the water could wash away the ache inside....

She closed her eyes, rested her forehead against the cool tiles, and let her thoughts return to the heart-rending scene at the pub.

While Grayson had made no move to touch her during

their whole conversation, she'd felt the tug, the invisible force drawing them together. After his surprise declaration, she'd been unable to speak for what seemed like ages.

There he was, opening up about his feelings for me, and all I could do was stare at him.

Her face crumpled and she banged her head against the wet tiles.

Being greeted by shocked silence must have been awkward, but he merely sighed and said I should take some time to think it over.

She wrapped her arms around herself.

But I didn't, did I? No, I had to blurt right there and then, 'Gray, I'm married. I can't just turn my back on that, despite—'

She doubled over, her forehead slipping down the tiles and bumping over the indented lines of grout.

I managed to say it, but every word felt like the stab of a blade.

Thrusting out a hand to stop herself sagging to the floor, she let the pain engulf her while the water tumbled over her neck and shoulders.

'He loves me,' her quivering lips whispered into the torrent of droplets, 'Grayson loves me, and I love him.' A sudden flood of warmth coursed through her, giving her the strength to lift her head and let the water wash the tears from her hot skin.

This man had made an effort to get to know her, and after only a short time knew her better than Troy ever would. They were meant to be together, she and Grayson. In her mind's eye seedlings emerged from what had been the barren garden bed of her life. All she had to do was tell him she'd changed her mind and this battle against their desires could be over, leaving them free to—

Free to do what? Have a sleazy, adulterous affair? I'd never sink to that, and neither would he.

The water continued to wash over her as the war once more raged between her heart and head. Their arguments had her melting with longing one moment, chilled and sad the next.

By the time she stepped out of the shower the inner battle was over. Her head had prevailed.

She had done the honourable thing. The answer she'd given Grayson was the only right one. Now she just had to live with it.

And that would be the hardest part.

Wednesday, 8:47:02 AM

    From: Maggie.Perkins@MRClonc

    To: Grayson.Reeves@MRMetro

    Copy to: Harry.Cochrane@MRClonc

    Subject: Conclusion of Cloncurry Relief

    Hi Grayson.

We note that your six week relief period ends this Friday. Please advise if you require any travel arrangements to be made for your return to Brisbane.

Regional Director Harry Cochrane has asked me to pass

on our appreciation for all your efforts on behalf of Cloncurry Office and its staff. It's been a pleasure working with you, and we wish you a safe journey home.

Best regards,

Maggie P

HR Advisor

MR Qld, Cloncurry

====================

Wednesday, 8:50:21 AM

From: Grayson.Reeves@MRMetro

To: Maggie.Perkins@MRClonc

Subject: Cloncurry Relief

Thanks Maggie.

My travel is all arranged. The fleet vehicle has been serviced and I'm right to leave on Saturday morning.

I'd like to thank you and Harry for your support and for giving me this opportunity to experience living and working out here, and the engineering team and other staff for making me feel so welcome.

I won't soon forget my time in 'the Curry'.

Kind regards,

Grayson Reeves

Acting Senior Civil Engineer, Construction

MR Qld, Cloncurry

====================

. . .

Late the following afternoon, when she looked through her internal office window to see Grayson striding purposefully up the hallway, Maggie had to quell an instant, unwarranted thrill. All the same, when he came into her office, closed the door and walked over to take a seat beside her, she shivered as though someone had put ice down her shirt.

'Maggie, I know I said I wouldn't—' Exhaling sharply, he dragged a hand over his head. 'But I have to make sure there's no way...?' He paused to gaze at her with silent appeal.

Her eyes roved over his face, his wide, beloved face with turned-down dark brows over grey-flecked hazel eyes, his feelings laid out there for her to see.

Acidic wretchedness rose to fill her throat.

Stay professional.

Stay professional.

Stay professional!

Taking a deep breath, she forced herself to speak. At her first attempt her voice broke, so she swallowed and tried again. 'I-I'm sorry things turned out ... like they did, Gray. It ... just has to be this way.' When her bottom lip quivered she pressed the top one over it, as her every atom silently begged him to accept the job and stay in Cloncurry.

She couldn't say it, though, couldn't tell him how she really felt. If he knew that, he was the type of man who'd stay and wait for her, which wouldn't be fair to him. And how on earth could she reconcile her marriage with him around? Resurrecting her relationship with Troy was what she needed to do ... wasn't it? Surely that was what her parents would expect her to do?

Bending to rest his elbows on his knees and clasp his hands together, Grayson looked down at the floor. 'I understand. And I respect your decision.' His voice was low, threaded through with emotion.

She tucked her own hands in her lap and let her gaze linger on him, drinking in every detail and committing them to memory.

When he raised his head and saw her eyes bright with tenderness and unshed tears, he turned away as though afraid of what he might do. Getting to his feet, he said gruffly, 'I ... I hope things work out for you, Maggie.' With a quick sideways glance he met her gaze, said softly, 'You deserve to be happy,' and strode out of her office.

Something shattered in his wake.

Shattered in her chest.

The hotel's lounge bar bustled with people come to farewell Grayson on his last night in Cloncurry. Maggie stood hesitantly just inside the door as Troy fought his way to the bar to order their drinks. She cast her eyes around the room until they alighted on the man of the moment. He was leaning with his back against the bar, gazing at her.

She managed to put something akin to a smile on her face and he did the same, only tearing his eyes away when Tom walked up to clap him on the shoulder.

'My shout, Reevers!'

Maggie watched the two men down their beers, glad

they'd become good mates but aching that she couldn't be part of that easy friendship. Her feelings for Grayson ruled out a platonic relationship, especially as they were reciprocated. Turning away sadly, she melted into the crowd.

When Troy pushed his way through the press of people toward her, he held their drinks high to stop the contents being spilled by a bump from a careless hand-talker.

She nodded her thanks as he handed her a glass, only to pull a face when she took a sip. 'Eeoo! What *is* this?'

'White wine,' came the offhand reply. 'That's what you wanted.'

'You didn't ask what *sort* it is?'

'Nope.'

'You know I like *dry* wine. This stuff's so sweet it could be straight cordial.'

He clicked his tongue. 'Look, it's the "house" white and it's cold, what more do you want?' Sauntering off to join a game of pool in the public bar, he left Maggie standing on her own and wishing herself somewhere else ... *anywhere* else. But she wouldn't be able to live with herself if she didn't farewell Grayson properly.

When she spotted Harry beckoning her, she gave a grateful smile and made her way across the room. As she drew close, he indicated Grayson with a lift of his chin and murmured, 'Shame you weren't able to convince him to take our offer.'

'Yes, after all the effort we went to it's ... a shame he's not staying.' Her voice sounded brittle to her own ears.

'Well, it was worth a try. I guess the bright lights of Brisbane would be hard to leave behind, 'specially for a single bloke. It can be lonely out here, on your own.'

'Mm.'

'Anyhow, I guess I'd better get this show on the road....' Moving to the centre of the room, Harry stood tall and tapped his glass until he had everyone's attention.

As he launched into his farewell speech, Maggie retreated to the back of the room, struggling to stem a flood of emotion.

Grayson's leaving.

I'll never see him again.

As the applause for Harry's speech subsided, Grayson stepped forward. Hearing the warmth in his deep voice as he spoke of his time in 'the Curry', Maggie swallowed, blinked back tears, and made herself stare at the scuffed floorboards at her feet. Her head jerked up when she heard him say, 'And I'd particularly like to thank Maggie, for introducing me to the joys of outback life, keeping me safe from cyclones, snakes, and gidgee bugs,' which caused a ripple of laughter through the room, 'and for helping make my time here memorable.'

Everyone turned to smile at her, but her gaze was fixed on the speaker and the unspoken message in the depths of his grey eyes.

Grayson worked his way through the remaining revellers until he got to where Maggie and Troy stood waiting to say their goodbyes. He shook Troy's hand and mumbled a few brief words, his eyes on Maggie the whole time. And when Troy moved away and she found herself standing alone with Grayson, it was almost Maggie's undoing. She clasped her hands behind her back and fixed a wan smile on her lips. When Grayson went to shake her hand, however, she surprised them both by stretching up to kiss him on the cheek.

Agonisingly aware others were watching, she made the caress a brief meeting of soft lips and firm warm cheek, a fleeting, bitter-sweet moment. As she made to draw away, Grayson put a hand at her elbow and bent his head to say in a low, gravelly voice, 'Take care of yourself, marvellous Maggie.' Straightening, he added with a lopsided grin that didn't meet his eyes, 'And good luck with the dancing spider search.'

She could only nod, blink rapidly, and give a sad, unsteady smile in return.

And that was it. Their final farewell was over.

Giving her elbow one last gentle squeeze, Grayson let his hand slip away as Troy came and took Maggie's arm. She paused to look at Grayson for one final, heart-rending second, and then silently accompanied her husband outside.

The air felt thick with the remainder of the day's warmth ... and so many unspoken words. Maggie rubbed both hands over her face to cover her shuddering sigh.

As they made their way wordlessly along the street toward home, she could hear Troy breathing as he walked beside her. Over their heads the ink of the night sky was broken only by the street lights, and farther above, the glitter of stars. As they passed the closed, silent post office down the street from its hotel namesake, a night creature scurried over the dry ground and into the safety of scorched foliage by the footpath, its rustlings loud in the heavy stillness.

When they reached their street corner Maggie couldn't resist looking back at the pub, where she saw Grayson on the footpath, illuminated by light streaming from the hotel's open double doors. He was standing with shoulders hunched, hands in the pockets of his jeans, staring after her.

She bit her lip until it bled.

17

Sunday, 3:35:56 AM
     From: Maggie.Perkins@home
To: Eviebird@myplace
Subject: Mind if I download on you ... again?

I'm miserable, Evie. Hardly eating or sleeping, not functioning normally at all. And I'm *horrible* to be around, all withdrawn and moody. I hate being like this but can't seem to jolt myself out of it.

When I go to bed, my dreams – when I *can* sleep – are all about loss. And when I'm awake, I feel sort of numb all the time. Even Troy's noticed I'm not myself. He's as sympathetic as usual, saying things like 'What's eating you?' and 'I'm a bit *over* all this moodiness'.

Guess I can't blame him, so I'm doing my best to perk up when he's around. After all, look at what I gave up for the sake of our marriage— Oh no! Why did I have to bring that up again?

Excuse me while I dissolve into tears for the umpteenth time....

It's like I'm sleep-walking through my life, Evie, and I need to wake up! Sure, I had a glimpse of how wonderful life could be – *truly* wonderful I suspect – but it's out of my grasp now Grayson has gone, so I have to put it all behind me and get over it. That's what I'm struggling with, letting go....

And I'm afraid I'll never be anything but sad from now on.

BTW, sorry I called so late the other night and kept you up so long, but who else can I talk to about this except you?

Maggie x

=====================

Monday, 10:38:12 AM

From: Eviebird@myplace

To: Maggie.Perkins@home

Subject: Re: Mind if I download on you ... again?

Hey luvvy, I'm worried about you – wish we didn't live so far apart. Sending you a BIG virtual hug. Now, warm-n-fuzzies over, let's get down to tin tacks. You need to buck up, girl! You'll make yourself sick the way you're going.

Look, I do still wonder why you and Grayson met and fell in love if it was all for naught, but if you're serious about making it work with Whatsisface, you're right, you *have* to let

Grayson go ... unless you're having second thoughts about you and Troy? *optimistic wink*

Okay, *okay,* don't give me that look! :(

I'm not trying to make this harder for you, but with your Mum and Dad not around I guess it falls to me to ask ... are you sure you're not flogging a dead horse? Pursuing a doomed union with Troy that should never have happened in the first place? And while you're thinking about that, also think on this: if they were here, would your folks want you to sacrifice a happy future for the sake of an unhappy marriage?

Just my two cents' worth.

From 'bad cop' Evie (with massive hugs).

xxx

BTW, email or call me ANY time.

=====================

Maggie closed Evie's email and slumped back against the pillows. Although she usually felt better after hearing from her friend, this time Evie had said something that was gnawing at her.

... would your folks want you to sacrifice a happy future for the sake of an unhappy marriage?

She let her head fall back against the bedhead as another memory sprang to mind, of coming home from a night out with friends to find her mother sprawled in a chair with her shoes kicked off, arms draped over the armrests and legs stretched out in front of her.

She looked up when Maggie came into the room. 'Just finished clearing away the dinner party debris.'

Maggie gave a fond smile. 'You're a glutton for punishment.' She dropped a kiss on her mother's head. 'Like a cuppa?'

'Oh yes, please.'

When Maggie handed her the steaming cup, Gwen dragged herself upright to wrap washing-up-reddened hands around it and sighed. 'I need this.' She took a sip. 'Ahh ... that's good,' and smiled warmly at her daughter. 'Thanks, love.' She took another mouthful. 'These social evenings can be hard work, especially if you don't get the right mix of people to keep the momentum going. And the Kerrs can be....'

'Boring?'

'Oh Maggie, that's not a nice thing to say. They just need more of a prod to get involved, that's all.'

'If you say so.'

'It's true.' Gwen sat forward to stretch her back. 'Ooh ... all that leaning over the sink, and lifting heavy pans from the oven....'

Maggie rose to massage her shoulders. 'You need to read that book, Mum.'

'What book?'

'The one called "Putting Backache Behind You".'

Gwen gave a tired laugh and then sobered. 'I wish you'd join us at more of our little soirees, love. You always add something special to the mix.'

'Sorry Mum, they're just not my scene. And over the years I've had more than my fair share of your culinary delicacies, like the infamous prune sandwiches.'

'Oh you! As if I'd serve sandwiches at a dinner party!'

'Well, well.' Maggie twitched an impish eyebrow. 'Good enough for your child but not your esteemed guests?'

Gwen gave an amused huff and leaned back in her chair. 'Speaking of the Kerrs, love?'

'Mm?'

'Sometimes people *think* they know what's right for someone else when, in reality, they don't.'

Maggie stifled a yawn. 'Yeah, so what's that got to do with the Kerrs?'

'Only that....' Gwen paused to take a breath. 'Just because someone – and by someone I mean *anyone,* including your father and me – thinks they know what *might* be good for you, love, that doesn't necessarily mean it *will* be.'

'I still don't know what you're getting at?'

'Sorry, I'm not being very clear. It's just that ... a bad decision made in haste can affect a person's whole life, and I'd hate you to feel obliged—'

Right at that moment, John Perkins bustled into the kitchen and pulled his groaning wife to her feet. 'Come on gorgeous lady.' He took her hand in his and put his other arm around her waist. 'I know what'll perk you up. You need a good dance!'

Despite her laughing protests, he waltzed her away to the tune of Gershwin's *I Got Rhythm* pumping from the lounge room stereo, leaving Maggie smiling indulgently and wondering what her mother had been trying to say. By the morning she'd forgotten to ask, and that was the end of it.

Too late she came to realise what her mother meant. By then she *had* felt obliged, *had* acted in haste, and was now 'repenting at leisure'.

'How about we take a holiday, Troy? Just the two of us.'

His eyes remained fixed on the TV. 'What for?'

'For fun – you remember what that is, don't you?' The cautious optimism in Maggie's voice wavered in the face of his lacklustre response. She perched on the arm of the couch and put a coaxing hand on his shoulder. 'We could go to Bali, or Vanuatu ... it'd be like a second honeymoon. What do you say, Troy? It'd be great, wouldn't it?'

'It'd be expensive.'

'Not necessarily.' She reached behind to grab a bundle of travel brochures from the hall table and placed them in his lap. 'I've sniffed out some good deals.' On the top brochure she'd pinned a note listing possible dates, flight options, costs, and even an itinerary. The note was dotted with smileys. As he picked up the bundle she watched his face, hoping to see a glimmer of interest. Instead he dropped the brochures on the chair beside him with a grunt.

Her face fell. 'Aren't you going to look at them?' The brightness was gone from her voice.

'Later.'

Sighing, Maggie got to her feet and trudged into the kitchen. She dug out some vegetables and began chopping them for dinner.

A few minutes later Troy came to sit at the breakfast bar, facing her. 'I know a good place for us to go.'

She looked up, her eyes bright with hope. 'Where?'

'Western Australia.'

Her shoulders slumped.

'We could take a holiday when we first arrive there, before I start the new job. And it wouldn't cost much at all. The company's paying our travel and relocation expenses. They're just waiting for me to confirm my start date.'

She bent her head and resumed chopping.

'Think what I'll be earning, Maggie. There'll be lots of money for holidays then.'

Without looking up, she said bleakly, 'And lots of time on my own while you're working overtime ... and without the benefit of a job to fill my days.'

'Aw, come on, Maggie. You'll find a job over there, think positive! This'll be a good move for us.'

She set down the chef's knife with a thud and wiped her eyes on her sleeves. 'Think positive, hey?' Her voice was harsh. 'Okay, how's this? I'm *positive* that we need to go away together, just the two of us, and soon. Somewhere there are no distractions like job offers, shift work, pig hunting – nothing but the two of us.'

'And I *agree* that we should go away together. To Western Australia.'

She gave an exasperated huff. 'Troy, you're not listening to me.' Waving away his annoyed mutter she plunged on, her voice steely. 'We need to concentrate on *us* for a change, and taking a *real* holiday together is the best way to do that.'

'*Us?*' He stared at her, clearly perplexed. 'What are you talking about? We're fine.'

'How can you say that? We need to work through this whole "move to WA" thing, but we hardly talk anymore. We squeeze our lives into tiny gaps around work and other commitments, and I spend so much time on my own I sometimes wonder if I *dreamed* our wedding. We need to connect with each other.'

'What do you mean, connect? I'm right here.'

'For now, but not for long. Soon it'll be another footy match on TV, or a hunting expedition with your mates, right before you head off on your next work shift.' She sighed. 'I need you to be my husband, Troy.'

'I don't get you. I *am* your husband.' His face darkened. 'And what about the other night when I wanted us to have dinner together, at home? It was *you* who had to go prancing off somewhere.'

'That was *once*, Troy! And it was business.' Her eyes glinted. 'You complain about being left on your own *one* time. What about all the time *I* spend alone?'

'You knew what it'd be like out here. You knew I'd be on shift work.'

'Yes, I did. What I *didn't* know was that you'd work every single bit of overtime offered, and spend most of what little free time you had with your mates, not your wife.'

He stuck out his chin and got down off the stool. 'Well, if that's the way you feel, I don't know why you'd want to go on a holiday with me.' Stomping, stiff-backed, to the lounge, he grabbed the TV remote control, turned up the volume, and flopped onto the couch.

When she saw him put his grubby feet on the bundle of brochures she'd so carefully put together, she squeezed her eyes shut and sighed. 'Troy, I...,' but he wasn't listening any more.

He hadn't been listening *at all*.

Tuesday, 11:12:17 PM

    From: Maggie.Perkins@home

    To: Eviebird@myplace

    Subject: The next instalment

Are you ready for the next instalment of the 'Tales of Miserable Maggie', Evie?

Remember I told you Troy wants us to move to WA so he can accept a job with BHP? Well, get this. Tonight he told me his flights are booked and he's leaving for Perth at the end of the week!

I'm sure you can imagine the row we had over that, but there's no stopping him. He's going, and there's nothing I can do about it.

He expects me to hand in my notice and join him over there once I've finished working out my termination period. I'll have to give up so much that's important to me to go with him, but what else can I do? He's my husband, for better or worse.

* head, desk, repeat *

Maybe I can put off the evil hour by giving a long period of notice, say six months. Harry would appreciate the extra time to find a replacement for me, and it would give Troy time to trial the new job. You never know, he might find he hates it and wants to move back! That's what happened when we came to Cloncurry, so it's not out of the question.

Oh Evie, as if my life wasn't complicated enough....

Maggie x

=====================

'Oh, thank goodness you answered this time, Evie! I couldn't *bear* to get your voice mail again. I don't mean to grouch, I'm just so....' Maggie paused to take a deep breath, pressing the receiver hard against her ear to stop it shaking. 'Give me a minute, I....'

At Evie's anxious enquiry she said quickly, 'Yes, yes, I'm okay. Just ... reeling from some shocking news.' She took another breath. 'You know how Troy promised to keep in touch while in WA? Well, he's only been gone a couple of weeks but I just checked our PO box and there was a letter from him. That was the first shock.' She went on in a nervous rush. 'Who would've thought he'd *write* to me? The odd email, phone call or text message, that was all I was expecting.'

After pausing to listen she said, 'It's only a short letter –

yeah, no surprises there, right? – but I must've read it at least ten times, to make sure....' Swallowing, she took a moment to moisten her lips. 'The biggest shock is what he enclosed with the letter.' She blinked hard. 'Legal papers, Evie. Troy wants a divorce.'

18

'You know I've been dragged in off the job to take this call?' The scowl was obvious in Troy's voice. 'They'll probably dock my pay.'

Thinking of the effort it had taken to reach him at the remote Western Australian mine site, Maggie had to bite back a stinging retort, instead saying tightly, 'I just got your letter.'

Silence.

'As I'm sure you can understand, it came as something of a shock.'

A grunt.

'I need you to confirm what you wrote, Troy.'

He swore, but softly as if there were ears nearby. 'Look, I sent you the legal stuff. You can read, can't you?' His tone was low and impatient.

Hers was even. 'I need to hear the words from your mouth.'

His long-suffering sigh whooshed from the receiver. 'Alright, if it stops you bothering me again. I ... want ... a ... divorce.'

'Why?'

'It's all in the letter.' His voice faded as if he were looking around, and then returned to normal volume. 'Do you *really* want me to spell it out for you over the phone?'

'No,' she said flatly, 'I suppose not.'

'Good, 'cos I've wasted enough time already. Are we done here?'

'Done? Yes ... we're done. And just so you know, I won't be contesting.' She hung up with a forceful stab of her finger on the button, and sat staring at the phone in her lap.

Was that typically blunt exchange of words to be her last conversation with her soon to be ex-husband?

She felt inside herself.

No twinge of sadness or loss, or even trepidation. Just ... a sense of closure and a need for action.

Setting her mouth in a firm line, she lifted the phone again.

Time to start the process of splitting their joint life into two separate pieces.

With the phone still pressed to her ear, Maggie moved higher on the stairs to get out of the sun's burning rays. Only half listening to Evie's excited ramblings, she eyed the much-read single sheet of grubby writing paper on her lap. Dotted with oily fingerprints, it bore a few scrawled paragraphs ... just enough words to sentence her marriage to death.

It was so like Troy to not waste words on things like feelings.

When Evie stopped to take a breath, Maggie went on. 'He says it was obvious I was stalling and had no intention of joining him in WA. Well, maybe I *was* stalling ... a bit ... but I was resigned to going, eventually. And it's not like I'd kept my feelings about the move to myself. I told him right from the start I didn't want to go.'

She paused to listen before continuing. 'And get this. About wanting us to split, he says....' Taking a quick scan of the page she read aloud, '... "I need to get some excitement back in my life again, after wasting so much time and effort on a boring marriage." Can you *believe* that? He's blaming *me*,' and she thumped an open hand against her chest, 'for the mess we made of things!'

This was greeted with some robust language as Maggie said sharply, 'And I'd like to know whose *efforts* he's talking about, and who he thinks made our marriage so boring.'

After letting Evie have her say she ventured, 'I think you could be right, he might've found someone else. If that's the case, to be honest I'm pleased for him, and I hope she – if there is a "she" – has better luck with their relationship than I did.'

She listened for a minute and then laughed aloud. 'Yes, won't he be thrilled if she expects to tag along on his footy trips and pig-hunting expeditions!' She sobered. 'Listen to me, will you? I sound happy, for the first time in ages. Should I feel guilty or glad about that?'

While listening to Evie's answer, she looked down and rubbed a foot absently over the cement stair. Her tone was sombre when she finally said, 'My husband has left me and is filing for divorce. Shouldn't I feel like the rug has been ripped out from under my feet? Instead I feel free, as if I can breathe again. Does that make me a bad person? Or does it simply prove that I never really loved Troy?' She nodded at Evie's response. 'That's true, our marriage *was* more like a prison sentence than a joyful union.'

After pausing to listen again, she blurted, 'No, I'm not going to call him, not yet. What would I say? "Hello, Gray. Troy's dumping me so can I change my mind about us?" That would be SO not fair to him, or me – or us, if there *is* an "us". Grayson deserves better than a pathetic rebound. I have to put the Troy chapter of my life behind me once and for all before I even *think* about starting another relationship.'

Her friend's response brought a slow, warm smile to her face. 'Thanks, Evie, and don't worry, as soon as the time's right, I *will* follow my heart. But I want my head to be happy about coming on that journey as well.'

Friday, 11:27:36 AM
　　From: Capability.Unit@MRMetro
　　To: Maggie.Perkins@MRClonc
　　Subject: Transfer at Level to Metro Office
　　Hello Maggie.

Further to recent discussions, we're pleased to inform you of a suitable Metro Office vacancy arising in the near future. This position is at your current level, so should you wish to be considered for it, you may submit a request to the Manager of the Capability Unit for a transfer at level.

We hope you decide to proceed, as we are all looking forward to having the chance to work with you.

Kind regards,

Bill Potts

Manager, Capability Unit

MR Qld, Brisbane

====================

Maggie closed the email and rested her chin on her hands. If she accepted the transfer, she could move to Brisbane.

And be near Grayson.

She felt the usual whole-body tingle, and then her forehead creased.

Harry would be disappointed. He hadn't bothered to hide his relief when she withdrew her resignation after receiving Troy's 'Dear Joan' letter. Coming around from behind his desk to shake her hand warmly, he'd said, 'I don't care why, Maggie, I'm just glad we're not going to lose you.'

She chewed her lip.

And how would Grayson feel about her being down there? Had he, like Troy, moved on in the months since they last saw each other, the months she'd taken to recover from the shock, work through the process of formalising the split with her husband, and rebuild the pieces of her life into something she could live with?

There'd been bad moments, of course, usually in the lonely stillness of night, when doubts crowded in to overtake her. Had she tried hard enough to keep her marriage together? Could she have done more? Would her parents have been disappointed by her failure?

And each time with the light of morning came the answers, always the same ones. She *hadn't* given up easily and *had* done everything she could think of to make it work. Her parents would've been proud of her for that, and for not being the one to deliver the fatal blow. For once, Troy had made a hard decision easy.

Taking out the business card Grayson had left on her desk with his home phone number written in a firm hand on the back, she held it against her heart. She'd managed to resist the temptation to call him despite having picked up the phone more than once, only to put it down again. Having sent him away, she wanted to make sure she was ready before inviting him back into her life.

They had exchanged work-related emails for a few days after his arrival back in Brisbane, and she took care to keep her responses friendly and professional, as with any colleague. Still, after the follow-up from his relief period had been completed, all claims finalised, requests granted and queries answered, leaving him no further reason to contact her, Maggie's heart ached at the absence of messages from him in her inbox.

That's what I wanted, time to sort myself out and draw a line under my marriage to Troy.

All the same, lying in bed at night – almost every night – she had to swallow her impatience and resist the impulse to reach for the phone. At times like that she reminded herself of how honourably he had acted toward her, and vowed to do right by him even if that meant delaying her own gratification. He deserved nothing less.

Maggie sat in the kitchen, hunched over yet another dinner-for-one, moving peas around the plate with her fork. She glanced longingly at the phone.

I have to wait for the *right* time to contact Grayson.

She frowned.

Hang on. What's wrong with now?

Her mind searched for an answer.

Nothing. Troy's in another relationship and I'm totally free to get on with my life.

Hope stretched gossamer wings inside her.

So what am I waiting for?

Her heart leapt. She dropped her fork with a clatter, sprang to her feet and raced to the bedroom, where she took out Grayson's business card from the drawer in her bedside table. Grabbing the cordless phone, she dialled his number with shaking fingers. The pounding of her heart filled her throat, making it difficult to breathe. She closed her eyes, eased her strangle-hold on the receiver, and tried to rein in her impatience.

Hurry up and answer, Gray. *Please.*

She heard a click and then a soft, sweet voice said, 'Hello?'

Maggie's stomach lurched and her lips froze in the 'O' position.

'Hello?' the woman said again, louder this time.

'Um ... h-hello.' Maggie licked her dry lips. 'Could I speak to Grayson please?' She looked down to see *both* her hands strangling the receiver.

'I'm sorry, he's out at the moment,' the woman said in a cultured British accent. 'Can I take a message? I'm his wife ... oops! ... ex-wife, Tina,' and she gave a tinkling laugh.

Maggie's stomach plunged to her toes. 'Oh ... right ... um ... no. Thanks. I'll ... um ... call back another time,' and she hastily hung up, to stare at the phone as if she'd never seen one before.

What is Grayson's ex-wife doing at his place, answering his phone?

A moan tore at her insides and the receiver slipped from her nerveless fingers.

Isn't it obvious?

19

'Here, drink this.' Tom handed Maggie a glass of brandy.

She looked at it and then back at him. 'I don't drink spirits, Tom, you know that.'

He pushed the hand holding the glass closer to her face. 'Take your medicine, young lady. You're as white as a ghost.'

She sighed and threw him a tight-lipped grimace, before closing her eyes and downing the brandy in one choking gulp. While she gagged and coughed, he studied her with concern.

Opening the door to her earlier that evening, he'd had to look twice to identify the unkempt woman on his doorstep. Now she sat in his lounge room, tell-tale streaks of congealed dust on her face, her normally neat hair in a scruffy pony tail, one corner of her shirt jammed into the waistband of her jeans, the other corner hanging loose.

He looked up when Lisa stepped quietly into the room. After greeting Maggie warmly, she exchanged a worried glance with her husband. 'I'll make us some tea. Give me a hand, will you love?' Once in the kitchen, she drew him close and whispered, 'The reality of the divorce must've finally hit her. I was afraid this might happen, she's taken it all too calmly.'

'You think that's what has upset her?'

'What else could it be?'

When they returned to the lounge room with the tray of steaming mugs, they took their time cautiously bringing the conversation around to Maggie's divorce. Their eyes widened when she shrugged off that subject as if it were of no conse-quence and then babbled something about Grayson having reconciled with his ex-wife. When their curious children wandered into the room, a mystified Lisa hurried them away to bed, after giving Tom a meaningful nudge.

He took the hint and moved to sit beside their visitor. 'So, tell me if I've got this right. You said ... you rang Grayson at home tonight, and his ex-wife answered the phone.'

Maggie gulped and nodded.

'And you're upset about that because...?'

She rolled her eyes. 'Tom, don't act dumb.'

'Excuse my dullness but I don't understand why that would get you in such a state, unless...?'

Seeing his raised brows, she said tartly, 'You *know* how I feel about him.'

'Well, I have some idea, but you've never actually said.'

'Oh?'

He nodded. 'So?'

She sucked in a deep breath, drawing strength from the fiery liquor in her belly. 'I love him, Tom.'

'Grayson. You're in love with Grayson Reeves?'

'Yep.' She cocked her head and said dreamily, 'Have been since I first met him, I think, but—'

'You were married to someone else.'

Her lips quivered and she gave a sad nod.

'And now that you're free?'

'I was hoping....' Her voice faded and she flicked him a sideways glance.

He eyed her thoughtfully before speaking again. 'Do you know how Grayson feels about you?'

'Well, I know how he felt just before he left here. As to what's happened since....' Her face fell.

'And how did he feel back then?'

'He said he'd take the job here and stay, but only if we had a future together ... me and him.'

'I see.' Sitting back in his chair, Tom took in her tousled, bent head and the way she was rubbing her upper arms as though chilled. She looked more like a miserable ragamuffin than her usual polished self. He leaned forward. 'You know, there are a lot of reasons why Grayson's ex might've answered the phone.'

She frowned up at him. 'Oh yeah? Apart from the obvious one, you mean?'

'Maybe she's just visiting.'

'Visiting her ex-husband?' she scoffed. 'Why on earth would a woman do that, unless she was hoping to rekindle the spark?' Her voice grew bitter. 'I hope Troy's not expecting *me* to visit *him* any time soon.'

Tom raised his hands in a pacifying gesture. 'Alright. But remember, we're talkin' about a Pom here. They're a different breed from us Aussies, so we shouldn't assume anything.' At her darkening countenance, he hastened to say, 'Not being derogatory, of course, just statin' the facts. Look, maybe there was a family emergency?'

'You're grasping at straws.' She gave a resigned sigh and slumped back in the chair. 'Let's apply the theory of Ockham's Razor, that the simplest explanation is probably the right one.' Taking a deep breath, she went on in a rush. 'Tina is at Grayson's place because they've reconciled, they're together again. And while I'm pleased for them....' She put a hand on Tom's arm. 'I really *am*, Tom, he deserves to be happy.' She let her hand slip away again. 'It means ... that ... I've missed my own chance ... at happiness....' Her voice broke as a sob rose from her belly, and her face crumpled.

Tom drew her into a bear hug. 'Oh Maggie, lass.'

Climbing out of the Gilmore's guest bed early the next morning, wincing and rubbing her head, Maggie slipped on the shirt and jeans she'd dropped on the floor the night before. Tom and Lisa had insisted she stay which was kind of them, but now she just wanted to be gone before they got up, so she didn't have to face them. She cringed. They'd assumed she was upset about the divorce, why hadn't she let them keep thinking that instead of laying out all her dirty laundry?

Because she'd drunk too much of that damn brandy....

She screwed up her face and pressed fingers to her temples.

I'll take some tablets when I get home.

After quickly making the bed, she opened the door and stepped into the hallway, taking care to move quietly.

As she tiptoed past the kitchen, Tom's voice made her jump. 'Like a cuppa, Maggie? I've got one here, ready.' He raised a steaming mug.

'No! Um ... no, thanks Tom. I'd better head home.'

'Are you sure you'll be okay?'

The kind concern in his voice made her face burn all the more fiercely. 'Thanks, I'll be fine.' She paused to fix him with an earnest gaze. 'And thanks for putting up with my babbling last night.' When he looked about to protest she hurried on. 'Please tell Lisa I'm sorry about the intrusion. I just ... needed to talk.'

'Don't apologise, girl. That's what friends are for.'

A ghost of a smile crossed her face. 'Anyway, thanks.' Seeing him about to rise from the kitchen stool, she waved him down. 'I'll let myself out. See you at the office.'

He watched her slip out the front door and pull it closed behind her with a soft click, as a sleep-rumpled Lisa emerged, wrapping a dressing gown around herself.

She yawned and took the mug of tea Tom handed her. 'Was that Maggie leaving?'

'Yep. She asked me to pass on her apologies about last night.'

Lisa's brow furrowed. 'What for? She didn't do anything wrong.'

'You know our Maggie, she doesn't like to be caught with her defences down. I think she was embarrassed.'

'But all she needed was someone to talk to, and who better than friends she can trust?'

'Yes....' His eyes narrowed and he pressed his lips together.

Lisa sipped her tea and peered at him. 'I know that look. What are you thinking?'

'Just that she needs more than someone to talk to.'

When he reached up to pull her onto his lap, Lisa rested her head on his shoulder and said sleepily, 'Tom Gilmore, I think you're planning something.'

'Far be it from me to interfere in affairs of the heart.' A slow smile spread across his face.

She glanced up at him. 'But?'

'I suspect a communication breakdown might be at the root of this problem.'

'And you think you can fix it?' She yawned again.

'Maybe. Worth a try, anyway.' Bundling his drowsy wife into his arms, Tom got to his feet and carried her into their bedroom, closing the door behind him with one foot.

20

'Bill Potts is coming here to meet with me tomorrow. Any chance you could pick him up from the airport?'

She looked up at him with raised brows and said slowly, 'Sure, Harry.'

'I know we usually get one of the junior officers to do the airport runs, but I'm hoping you'll have a quiet word with Bill in the car, give him a heads-up about our current staffing issues. He'll want names in some cases, and if you give them to him in advance – and in private – I can avoid having to mention them in my discussions with him.' He scowled. 'You know how the walls have ears around here.'

She gave a rueful nod. 'He'll be on the four-thirty flight?'

'Yep. Thanks Maggie.'

As she watched Harry head back along the corridor to his office she frowned and sucked on her lower lip.

So ... Bill's coming here tomorrow. I wonder if he's

mentioned anything to Harry about the metro position I've been offered.

She brooded on the implications of that, and then decided it was time for a caffeine injection. Although the lunch room was empty, she could hear muffled voices in the training room next door, a departmental Code of Conduct session she had arranged for some recent starters. While distractedly rinsing her cup under the hot tap, she stared moodily through the window into the covered courtyard, and caught a flicker of movement on the ground.

The slender Gilbert's Dragons, known locally as 'Tat-ta' lizards, were becoming active again. One bold fellow scampered across the paving and climbed nimbly onto a rock to strike a pose not unlike a willowy super model. He sat waving a dainty arm in a circular motion as though in greeting, before darting back into the shrubbery. Maggie was only vaguely aware of the performance. She stood wiping her already squeaky-dry mug over and over, eyes fixed on a faraway point.

While I'm having that 'quiet word' with Bill, I'll also let him know I won't be applying for the transfer after all. What would be the point now?

After finally making herself a coffee, she stood stirring it for whole minutes.

I could still go, I 'spose. Maybe it's time I returned to city life? There are always promotion opportunities in Metro, so it would be a good career move too. Guess I need to think about things like that now I'm on my own.

And I'd still be on my own in Brisbane, so do I *really* want to up-stakes and move somewhere I don't know anybody?

Well ... I'd know somebody, but he's....

A familiar ache arose. Wrapping both hands around her mug, she took a sip and wrinkled her nose. The coffee was already cooling. She'd forgotten to pre-warm the milk, and all her stirring had dissipated much of the water's heat. With a resigned sigh, she tipped the luke-warm coffee into the sink and watched it circle the basin before finally draining away.

Gone ... with no hope of retrieval.

She drew a deep, tremulous breath and straightened.

Better get back to work.

———

'Hey Reevers, it's Tom.'

'Tom?' Grayson's voice at the end of the line held a warm welcome. 'To what do I owe the pleasure?'

'Just ringin' to see how life's treatin' you.'

'Good thanks cobber. And what about you? And Lisa and the kids?'

'We're all fine.'

'And what about...?'

'Yeah?'

Grayson hesitated before saying quickly, 'The staff up there. How are they all doing?'

Tom gave a roguish grin. 'Good, mate. All good.'

Silence, then Grayson said gruffly, 'So ... what's been happening?'

Tom launched into a status update. 'Well, we've started on that project you instigated....'

'Right, I think that's about it.'

Grayson gave an approving grunt and then said, 'What about Chandra's promotion?'

'Looks promising, thanks to your recommendation. Oh, and he and his wife are expecting a baby.'

'Give them my congratulations.'

'I will.'

A pregnant pause followed. Finally Tom said, 'Say, I tried ringin' you at work a while ago and was told you were away on leave?'

'Yes, I just got back the other day.'

'Where'd you go?'

'Home, to the UK.'

'Oh yeah? A holiday, or something else?'

'Family business. I had an S O S from Mum—'

'An S O S? I hope everything's okay?'

'It is now.'

'What was the emergency?'

'Remember I told you things weren't good between my brother and father?'

'Mm.'

'Well, it came to a head with bouts of yelling and some push-and-shove, which I would've liked to have seen – neither of them is what you'd call a prize fighter.' Grayson gave an amused huff. 'Dad used to be handy but he's getting on, and Mark's normally a gentle giant. Anyway, they had Mum at her wits' end, so she rang me. There wasn't much I could do from here, so I decided to take some leave and go over there to sort it out.'

'And did you?'

'Between me and Mum, yes. Turns out Mark's done some good things with the money I'd lent him, so his horticulture business is thriving. Dad was still being critical of his 'stupid' choice of career so Mark tried to tell him how well he was doing, but the old man wouldn't listen, didn't want to hear he was wrong and Mark was right. Dad can be a stubborn old coot with a mean turn of phrase when he gets riled. And he must've been in really good form to get Mark angry enough to have a go.'

'What'd you do?'

'Nothing too drastic. I just sat them both down – threatened to drag Dad to the table by the scruff, which didn't go over too well but got him there – and *made* them talk it through. This time he *had* to listen to Mark. Then, after he'd calmed down and realised he can boast to his old-boys brigade that both his sons are doing well, we all went to the local for a few lagers. Later, I laid some other home truths on him, like the fact we're not just his sons, we're men, and need to follow our own paths in life. I think he was already coming to terms with that on his own, just needed a push to get him over the line.'

'Nicely done. So tell me, you weren't tempted to stay over there?'

'In the UK? No mate, Australia's my home now.'

Tom chuckled at his use of the term 'mate'. 'And you didn't bring anyone back with you?'

'No ... but Mum's keen to come for a visit one day soon.'

'And no other female travelling companion?'

'What?'

'Just wondering if a certain woman might be back in your life now.'

'A woman?' There was a frown in Grayson's voice and his tone grew wary. 'What makes you ask that?'

'So that's a no?'

'Get to the point, Tom.'

'I'm asking if you're seeing anyone.'

'*Seeing* anyone? No, but— Look, what's this all about?'

'Sorry, I know this is none of my business, but ... how do you feel about Maggie? Maggie Perkins.'

'Maggie?' After a heavy silence Grayson said stiffly, 'She's a nice person, and a colleague.'

'Is that all she is to you?'

'I....'

'Honestly now, Reevers. I need to know.'

Those words.... Hadn't his mother said something similar?

At the end of her tether thanks to the long-running and escalating upset between her 'pig-headed' husband and their sensitive youngest son, Elizabeth Reeves was at first relieved and then concerned when her eldest arrived home from

Australia. She could tell he was hurting, despite the passage of time since his split with Tina.

It was so like her gallant, steadfast son to hold solidly to the things that mattered.

She thought back to that worrying time. Still teary after their farewell, she had been picturing the couple en route to Australia, imagining them too excited to sleep on the long-haul flight, when Tina's mother rang to tell her what had transpired at Heathrow. Immediately anxious for her son, Elizabeth had risked her husband's ire by making a number of expensive international calls to Australia until she managed to reach Grayson. After they spoke briefly she judged him to be emotionally flattened – naturally – but resigned, and dealing with the situation in his own self-sufficient, manly way.

Elizabeth knew her boys better than anyone. She admired Grayson's strength of character and independent 'I'll handle it' approach to life. He was her go-to when she needed help, like with the worsening situation between Mark and his father. So it dismayed her to see her big, strong, capable eldest son sitting at her kitchen table hunched over, silent and withdrawn.

What was going on with her family? Were they *all* falling apart?

She gave him time to recover from jet lag and then, when the other two men were out the next morning, she put a mug of tea in front of him and asked outright if he was nursing a broken heart.

He didn't reply so she sat beside him, rested her head on

his broad shoulder, and gently asked how he was coping without Tina. When he still didn't speak she urged, 'Honestly now, Grayson. I need to know.' She rarely used his name, mostly called him 'love', so she knew that would get his attention.

She was greeted first with a frown and then a resigned sigh. Finally he said gruffly, 'Tina and our broken marriage are old news. I've put all that behind me.'

Her eyes widened and she studied his face. 'Really?'

He nodded, and she could see he was telling the truth.

She sat back to gaze at him. 'So, why do you look so ... miserable?'

He sighed again, and then went on to tell her about a girl he'd met in Australia, a girl he'd fallen for ... but shouldn't have.

Elizabeth sat quietly watching the emotions crossing her son's face. She could see the depth of his feelings for this Australian girl.

If only she could've been British. Oh, to have her eldest back in the UK again....

Elizabeth took a breath.

More important that he be happy.

Rubbing his arm consolingly, she said a silent prayer that her son and this girl work out whatever was holding them back from being together....

'Reevers, you still there?'

'I'm here.' He exhaled. 'Look, Tom, what I feel for Maggie is immaterial. She's married to someone else.'

'Just humour me, will ya? I'll tell you why in a minute.'

Grayson didn't speak for a few seconds. Then he said slowly, 'Alright, because it's you, Tom, and I trust you not to mention this to anyone.' He paused. 'I have ... feelings for Maggie. But—'

'And there's no other woman in your life?'

'Not in that way, no.'

'Not even the hoity-toity Ms Tina?'

'We're divorced, you know that.'

'So there's no way she could've answered the phone at your place?'

'She what? Well, actually....' He sucked in a breath and Tom could almost hear the cogs whirring in his brain. 'Who's been trying to ring me at home, Tom?'

'Never mind. What about Tina?'

'You'd better be going somewhere with this.'

'I am. Answer the question.'

Grayson's exhalation whooshed down the phone line. 'Tina and her new hubby, Nolan, are in Australia on holiday, and they called in to see me the other evening. I nipped out to pick up a bottle of wine, and when I got back Tina said a woman had rung while I was out—'

'How did that go, the visit I mean?'

'I wasn't sure what to expect, but it turned out to be okay. I even managed to resist the temptation to punch Nolan's lights out. To be honest, he doesn't seem like such a bad chap. Even apologised to me for his part in our split. Said he was so in love with Tina, he forgot his principles for a while. They're happy together, so I guess all's well that ends well.'

'How do you feel about that?'

'I'm pleased for them.' Tom heard the dismissive shrug in Grayson's voice.

'So, no regrets, mate?'

'None at all. Tina leaving me was the best thing for both of us.'

'But visiting you … isn't that an odd thing for an ex-wife to do?'

'I thought so too, until she explained the reason for the visit.'

'Which was?'

'To apologise in person for the way she'd ended things, and to share their good news. They're expecting their first child.'

'I see.'

'So, are you *finally* going to tell me what this is all about?'

'Yeah.' Tom's voice grew solemn. 'Reevers, there's something I think you should know. Now, I'm only telling you this because I trust you not to hurt someone I care about….'

When Tom finished telling him of Maggie's split with Troy, her phone call to him and her distress after Tina answered the call, Grayson said brusquely, 'Thanks, Tom, I owe you,' and hung up.

As he slowly replaced the receiver, Tom murmured, 'Gilmore, out. The rest is up to you two.'

21

The fleet vehicle bumped over the uneven road surface as Maggie took the turn to the airport. She'd lost count of the times she'd been there – collecting travellers or travelling herself – but was still struck by the contrast of the bare earth's deep orange-red with the clear blue outback sky, made more obvious by the open expanse.

It seemed she'd never tire of admiring the area's distinctive 'outbackness'.

There was none of that in Brisbane, just acres of skyscrapers, roofs, and bitumen.

She pressed her lips together.

All the more reason to stay put....

As she passed the corrugated iron hangar with *Original Home of Qantas* painted on it in large red letters, she felt the usual swell of pride at the important part Cloncurry, the town 'out the back of whoop-whoop' and her home, had played in Australia's history.

After parking the car in a swirl of red dust, she walked into the tiny terminal building.

'G'day, Maggie. Goin' somewhere or just pickin' up today?' Airport managers Jack and Mabel had a friendly though efficient 'country yokel' attitude that endeared them to everyone passing through the terminal's doors.

'G'day Jack. Just another ViP, up from Briz.'

'Gettin' the full treatment ay, havin' the likes of you to pick 'im up?'

'Thanks for the compliment.'

He grinned and then said, 'The four-thirty's runnin' a few minutes late, love, so 'ave a seat. Wanna cuppa?'

'No, thanks. Think I'll wait outside.'

Mabel popped her head around the corner from where she was stacking the baggage cart. 'Hot out there, darl.'

'Of course.' Maggie managed to share a smile with her, and then pushed open the glass doors to walk out of air-conditioned coolness into a wall of hot air.

She squinted in the dazzling glare off the runway and ambled to the arrivals gate, to stand in the warm breeze, staring across the flat landscape surrounding the airport. Shading her eyes with a hand, she glanced up and saw a pair of eagles coasting on air currents far above.

At the memory of the wedge-tails she and Grayson had encountered on their trip to the gulf, she blinked as an all-too-familiar ache settled in her heart. She turned away, to watch another car pull into the dusty carpark and disgorge passengers, all dressed in high-vis mining workwear.

When her ears picked up a drone from above, she scanned the sky and saw the sun glint off the QantasLink Dash Eight. She waved away a pesky fly and watched the twin-prop plane approach the runway, slowly losing altitude, at times appearing to hang suspended in the air. She wondered idly how many passengers were on board. With few airlines servicing the remote routes, the flights were often fully booked.

Her mobile phone chimed and she pulled it out of a pocket. 'Hello?'

'Maggie, it's Tom.' From the background noise she knew he was calling from a car phone.

'Oh, hi Tom.'

'Where are you?'

'At the airport.'

'WHAT?'

She held the phone away from her ear and frowned. What was up with *him*? Why was he so shocked about her being at the airport? She put the phone to her ear again. 'Ah ... Tom, are you okay?'

'Yeah, sorry Maggie. I ... um ... what are you doing at the airport?'

'Picking up Bill Potts, from Capability in Brisbane.'

'Oh. He's on the four-thirty?'

'Yep.'

This met with a drawn-out silence.

'I don't mean to be rude, Tom, but *you* called *me*. Did you want something?'

'Ah ... well ... no. Nothing that can't wait.'

'Oh. Okay then. Well, I'd better go, the plane's about to land.'

'Yeah ... right ... seeya.'

First he's shocked and now he's *amused*? What's going on with him?

She gave a bemused frown. 'Bye, Tom.'

Turning, she watched the gleaming, streamlined machine land smoothly on the searing tarmac with a squeal of tyres and a roar of engines. It slowed and turned at the end of the runway to coast to the front of the terminal building.

Thinking it was lucky she knew Bill Potts and didn't have to hold one of those embarrassing name boards, she made her way to the arrivals gate.

In a flurry of activity, airport staff prepared to receive the arrivals, replenish and check the aircraft, and board the waiting passengers for the return journey.

Maggie stood to the side of the gate, where she was quickly surrounded by others waiting to collect friends, colleagues, loved ones.

Young people chatted excitedly while watching for their friends to emerge; mothers and children waited impatiently to greet husbands and fathers; and standing close by the gate with her fingers threaded through the wire, a young woman in a red dress kept her eyes locked on the plane as though desperate for the first glimpse of ... the man she loved?

Seeing the longing on the young woman's face, Maggie swallowed the lump in her throat and looked away.

She was sick of the perennial ache in her heart.

Sick of weeping for squandered chances, disappointments, and out of sheer loneliness.

Sick of longing for something she couldn't have.

The whine of the plane's engines broke into her thoughts, as the aircraft nosed into position close to the terminal under the direction of Jack's paddles.

Maggie watched the propeller blades turn from a blur of motion into separate points again as the pilot shut down the engines. Jack then chocked the wheels, rolled out the air stairs, and climbed them to knock on the cabin door. It was opened from within and the stewardess greeted him with a broad smile.

Maggie was watching the first passengers disembark when a tap on her shoulder made her spin around. Tom stood behind her, grinning.

'What are *you* doing here, Tom?'

'Same as you.'

'Oh? So who are you meeting?'

'A friend.' There was an air of mystery about him.

She decided not to ask, just threw him a smiling frown and then turned to watch the long line of passengers make their way across the hot tarmac.

She spotted Bill Potts among them, and then glimpsed a familiar-looking tall physique in a polo shirt further back in the line. It was so like Grayson she gasped and turned away, her nerve endings stinging as though doused in hot caustic.

Not here. Not now. I mustn't make a fool of myself.

She put a hand to her forehead.

I have to stop 'seeing' him everywhere, in groups of people, disappearing around corners, in every second car I pass. I'm creating my own personal torture chamber.

She squeezed her eyes shut and took a deep breath before turning back to see Bill at the gate, a hand raised in greeting. She was forcing a smile on her face when her eyes were trapped by an intense gaze from over Bill's shoulder. It originated from a pair of grey-flecked hazel eyes, in a wide face whose dark brows turned down at the inner edge as though frowning....

Hearing Maggie suck in a sharp breath, Tom's grin widened. He moved closer, ready to catch her if her knees gave way.

Bill was walking up to her, hand extended. When she didn't take it, just stood as though cryogenically frozen and stared wide-eyed past him, he frowned.

About to ask if she was alright, he felt himself shoved aside by a tall man in a red polo shirt, who mumbled, 'Scuse me, sir,' as he moved to stand close to Maggie.

She didn't budge, speak, or even breathe as Grayson gazed down at her. When he reached up a hand to brush back a strand of hair fluttering around her face, she closed her eyes and rested her cheek in his warm palm.

That was all the signal he needed. Pulling her into his arms, he whispered into her hair, 'Maggie, love.'

Awestruck, disbelieving, and joyous all at once, she said breathily through lips pressed against his shirt, 'Oh, Gray.'

While on the plane he'd practiced what he would say to her, going over and over the different versions in his mind. But when the time arrived, it was the simple message that came to him.

Uncaring who else would hear, he said in a deep voice that broke a little, 'I love you, Maggie.' Keeping hold of her, he pulled away just enough so he could look her in the eyes. 'Are you free to love me back?' He held his breath.

'Yes.'

Exhaling in a rush, he pulled her close again, resting his cheek on the top of her head.

Her next words were muffled breaths against his broad chest, but he heard them and his heart rejoiced at every syllable. 'I can say it now. I *love* you, Grayson.'

Drawing back, he took her face in his hands. Her eyes glistened with glad tears, and in their depths he saw hopes, dreams and a wonderful future, and he could hold back no longer. He bent his head as she wrapped her arms around his neck, her pleading lips succumbing joyously to his kiss as the rest of the world faded into oblivion.

A few of the milling passengers tittered at the romantic scene playing out in front of them, and some burst into gentle applause. All Maggie knew was that she'd finally arrived at her destination.

She'd negotiated all the road blocks, barriers and potholes on the long road to loving Grayson.

Tom was still beaming when his eyes fell on Bill Potts, who stood staring open-mouthed at the heart-warming scene. Stepping forward to grasp his hand, Tom gave it a vigorous shake. 'G'day mate, and welcome to Cloncurry. Been a change of plan, I'll be your driver today.'

As he led the way to the car he saw Potts glance back at the loving couple, and grinned. 'Yep, it's not called the warm heart of Australia for nothin', ya know.'

If you've enjoyed reading **The Long Road to Loving Grayson***, I hope you'll consider posting a review on your retailer's site and/or on Goodreads - Maggie and Grayson will love you for it!*
Alicia :)

ANOTHER IN THE LONG ROAD SERIES

The Long Road to Loving Jackson

The second in the LONG ROAD series, with more to come.

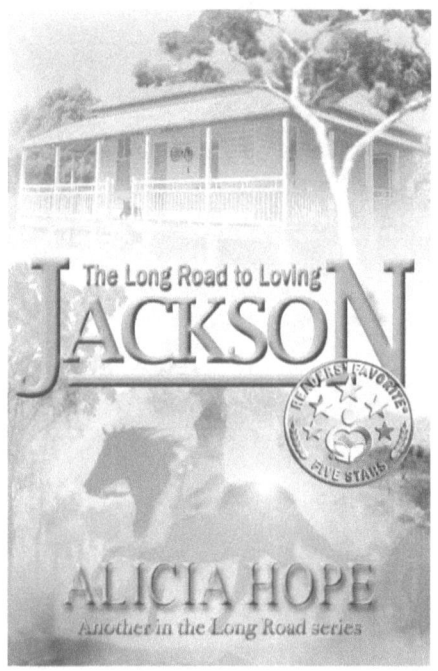

On the long road back from tragedy, trick rider Abbey limps home to the farm only to be confronted with more strife, and a tough choice. Should she cut and run or stay and ride it out?

Sometimes life offers a second chance and for the lucky, more than one. And on a long road, it can be the hitchhikers we collect along the way that make the journey worthwhile.

The Long Road to Loving Byron

If castle walls could speak, what secrets would they tell?

To solve an age-old mystery tainting her family's past, Aussie Claire-Rose must brave a New Zealand castle's gloomy halls, delve into ancient history, and unearth more than one long-hidden secret. Things get complicated when a life-altering calamity follows her across 'the ditch', and even more so when she crosses paths with the castle's handsome co-owner....

ALSO BY ALICIA HOPE

The Cafe Birds

Literal chick lit!

A no-fail recipe: in five pretty cafés, blend women friends and their modern day dramas with to-die-for coffees and scrumptious cakes, and serve.

Bon appétit.

A NOVELLA BY ALICIA HOPE

Sisters of War

A tale of love, betrayal and courage in wartime Austria. Of five
women who lived, loved, and lost under the ever-watchful eye of
the Third Reich.

MEET THE AUTHOR

Once you choose HOPE anything is possible....

You can connect with Alicia online at
http://www.aliciahopeauthor.blogspot.com